# Quiet Walks the Tiger

***Also by Heather Graham
in Large Print:***

Tender Taming
When Next We Love
Lord of the Wolves
Queen of Hearts
Spirit of the Season
A Season for Love

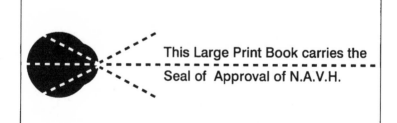

This Large Print Book carries the
Seal of Approval of N.A.V.H.

# *Quiet Walks the Tiger*

## Heather Graham

**Thorndike Press • Thorndike, Maine**

Published in 2001 by arrangement with Leisure Books, a division of Dorchester Publishing Co., Inc.

Thorndike Press Large Print Famous Authors Series.

The tree indicium is a trademark of Thorndike Press.

The text of this Large Print edition is unabridged. Other aspects of the book may vary from the original edition.

Set in 16 pt. Plantin.

Printed in the United States on permanent paper.

**Library of Congress Cataloging-in-Publication Data**

Graham, Heather.
    Quiet walks the tiger / Heather Graham.
        p.  cm.
    ISBN 0-7862-2519-X (lg. print : hc : alk. paper)
    1. Married women — Fiction.   2.Large type books.
    I. Title.
PS3557.R198 Q48 2001
    813′.54—dc21                                    00-025198

*For Dennis*

*For Mom  
with many thanks*

# PROLOGUE

Grace, poise, and magic . . . she was all of these, the epitome of all the beauty that the physical body of woman could be. She had been born to dance, her body trained to utilize the natural talent to the utmost. As she swayed and dipped and swirled, the muted lights enhancing the unusual mixture of brunette, red, and gold that mingled in her flowing hair, she was a creature in her element. The music was in her slender form, a goddess sheathed in a shimmering bath of violet-tinged clouds. The love of the music, the instinct to follow it, glowed radiantly in her face. It touched her feet until it seemed she flew, no servant to the laws of gravity. She allured and enticed as she danced, emitting a message as old as pagan ritual, as natural as man himself.

To most who watched her, she was simply a part of the magic of the evening, a striking member of the prestigious Fife Dance Company. They would go home and remember the enchantment of the theater, the fascination of the dance, and then take off their gloves and cloaks and bask in pleasant memory until another night out in dress-up enlivened the monotony of day-to-day life. They would think of those on stage as something more than mortal, incredible beings of sheer physical perfection. They would shake their heads and momentarily wish that they too were so agile, so taut of muscle, so fleet of foot. They would envy without thinking of the endless years of commitment and work, and then they would forget.

One man in the audience would not forget. He knew the woman who had taken center stage, exhibiting the full and intoxicating physical expression that was dance.

He had come because of her. He didn't plan to try to talk to her; he just came to see her. He knew she was married, and because of the man he was, he truly wished that marriage all the luck in the world. But he was in love with her. They had dated only once, but that one night had hopelessly entangled him. She had invaded his bloodstream and dreams ever since.

He was a bit like an out-of-date Lancelot, he told himself ruefully as he watched the performance. She belonged to another, but she held his heart. And so he was sworn to her, to love and forever cherish her from afar.

He wasn't at the theater alone, and he knew his companions would have a hell of a laugh if they knew what went on in his mind. He and the two with him were also creatures of physical perfection — a different kind, and at the moment, more famous than any of those on the stage would ever be.

They were football players and the backfield of the team that had just won one of the greatest American quests for glory — the Super Bowl.

And here he was — the macho, rugged leader of the pack — the quarterback, mooning over a slip of a girl who moved like quicksilver over a stage. . . .

The performance ended. The three tuxedoed men in the audience, friendly giants of virility, were asked for as many autographs as the dancers.

Backstage the girl changed. She hadn't a single thought of the audience on her mind; she was anxious to see her husband. She had marvelous news for him. Intimate, wonderful news. They were expecting their first child.

The football players were heading for a party. He might have sworn his heart to her

. . . but hell, a man had to live. . . .

He wouldn't remember the name of the woman he was with that night or the color of her hair. But he was gallant. He always was. Charm was as much a part of his nature as power and the innate magnetism that drew respect from men and women alike. . . . He had a good time at the party.

He didn't see his dancer until five years later. And on that occasion he remained in the background again, although his heart was breaking for her.

She was a solemn figure that day, ramrod straight and proud. Slim and hauntingly beautiful in black.

The last earthly remains of her husband were interned into the earth. Ashes to ashes, dust to dust. She was surrounded by people who loved her, but she would be led away by none. She stayed as the first shovels of earth fell on the coffin. She stood straight and unyielding until she was alone.

Then her knees buckled and she fell to the carpet of green grass that encircled the mound of newly dug earth. Her hands flew to her face, and even from his distance he could hear the terrible sobs wracking her slender frame.

He knew he couldn't go to her; he knew

he couldn't help her. He just stood there, railing against his helplessness, watching until the sun sank in a burst of crimson behind the hills.

It would be another two years before he would go to her.

# CHAPTER ONE

The band in the dinner lounge was really very good. They were versatile and had done everything from Sinatra to Blondie and managed to complacently oblige almost any request for a song from the thirties to the eighties — spacing them to please the young hard rockers and the mature dinner clientele.

Sloan Tallett had been on the dance floor, twirling beneath the lights, for the majority of the evening. She was a beautiful woman, never more regal than when on a dance floor, and with her escort being the head of the dance department from the college where she taught, she had provided the patrons of the lounge with visual entertainment as well as acoustical. Eyes riveted and stayed upon the handsome couple, which was what Jim Baskins intended. They were the best advertising he could manage for the College of Fine Arts.

The number, a breath-stealing piece from the late sixties, came to a halt. Sloan laughed gaily to Jim as they wove their way to their table, hand in hand. She was flushed as she sat, her blue eyes as radiant as sapphires. Someone stopped by to issue a compliment, and she smiled with lazy thanks, the full-lipped, seductive smile of a temptress.

She had been born to dance — her friend and escort was thinking — but she had also been born to captivate. Only someone close could ever see the hard line of reserve and pain that lurked beneath the stars in her eyes and the radiance of her smile.

"Another scotch and soda?" Jim asked.

"No!" She chuckled, but her answer was firm. She glanced at her black-banded wristwatch with a frown. "It's too close to pumpkin time, I'm afraid. I'd love a plain soda, though, with a twist of lime."

"I'd probably better order the same," Jim said with a grimace, motioning to their waitress. "You're good for me, Sloan, do you know that?" he said after putting their order in. "You keep me on the straight and narrow."

Sloan smiled at her companion. Jim Baskins was twenty years her senior, and she was sure he had traveled the straight and narrow all his life. He was her immediate supervisor, and a more gentle, understanding

13

man couldn't be found. A confirmed bachelor, Jim had dedicated his life to two demanding mistresses — dance and teaching. Approaching fifty, he had the look of a much younger man. An inch or so over Sloan's five feet seven inches, he was thin and wiry, the touches of silver in his thick blond hair adding an air of distinguished maturity. Most people who saw them together decided there was a romantic interest between the two — which wasn't true. They were co-workers and friends who enjoyed one another's company.

"I think it's the other way around," Sloan told him. "You keep me on the straight and narrow."

"Two damn straight and narrow, if you ask me," Jim replied. "You should be dating, Sloan. You're a young woman, and it's been two years . . ." His voice trailed away; he hadn't meant to remind her of the husband he had never met.

Clouds passed over the sapphire of her eyes, but Sloan kept smiling. "It's all right, Jim. It has been two years since Terry died. And I do date occasionally. When I'm interested. But society has picked up a little too much for me. Every time I date someone a second time, they seem to think I've said yes to hop into bed."

"It wouldn't kill you to have an affair," Jim advised, surveying her over his soda. "And you should consider a second marriage —"

"I don't want to marry again," Sloan interrupted softly. She had had a good marriage, and anything shallow to follow would be sacrilege. She looked at Jim to see him, miserable, before her and realized she was extending her own unhappiness to him. And she wasn't really unhappy. She had her job, she had the children. "Why would I want to marry?" she queried cheerfully. "I have enough of my own problems! I don't need someone else's!"

Jim didn't look quite so miserable. "Bad attitude, Sloan. You share the good along with the bad."

Sloan laughed easily. "Jim — it's not something I have to decide immediately. I don't exactly have a score of suitors pounding down my door. You'd have to be a rich man to contemplate marriage to a struggling thirtyish widow with three children age six and under. Come to think of it, you'd have to be a lunatic as well."

"I'd marry you, Sloan," Jim said softly.

Sloan chuckled softly and stretched slender fingers across the table to envelop his hand. "You are a lunatic," she told him with warm affection. "And I do believe you mean it." Jim was aware that her life was rough — finances were low, and her job schedule, while trying to be a good mother to three young children, was grueling. "But I love you as a very dear friend, as you love me — and like I said, I don't want to get married. I'm a very independent lady — I run my own life."

Jim shook his head sadly. "You're a beautiful woman, Sloan. Someday some man is going to come along and crumble that shell of yours — and I hope I'm around to see the day."

"Only if he has a fortune!" Sloan teased. "Come on, boss," she added, rising. "Walk me to my car. I don't like to keep Cassie waiting. She expects me home no later than ten."

Sloan's sister kept her children on Friday nights so that Sloan could have an evening out. Usually, it was dinner and dancing with Jim or the occasional date that intrigued her. Friday nights were her only fling. She needed them to remind herself that she was still shy of thirty, still young. She enjoyed her evening with Jim and the few "real" dates she accepted, but that was as far as she would venture from the wall she had carefully built around herself after Terry's death.

Life was too serious a thing for her to take the time to really unscramble her feelings on love, sex, and affairs. It was — at this point — a fight for survival.

"Okay, gorgeous," Jim said amicably, signaling for the check. "We'll get you in for curfew. It's supposed to be twelve, though — not ten," he teased, dropping a few bills on the table and rising to assist her from her chair. "But I guess it's about the same. 'Beautiful, sexy, seductive dancer goes home and turns back into household drudge!' "

"Thanks," Sloan said dryly, grinning as she accepted his arm. "Just what every woman needs. A boss with a sense of humor."

Jim guided her from the still-thriving lounge to the parking lot. Since they could shower and change in the dance department, they went out straight from work, and both had their own cars. Courteous as always, Jim saw her into her Cutlass and closed and locked the door for her.

"Beautiful night," he mused, sticking his well-kept frame, nicely suited in a double-breasted jacket, through her window. "You should be enjoying it with some nice knight in white armor."

"I had my knight!" Sloan said with a

wistful smile. "They don't come charging through a life twice — there is a shortage of white horses!"

"You're a cynic, Sloan," Jim said with a shake of his head. "Grown hard as nails."

"Oh, Jim!" Sloan protested, smiling. "I'm not a complete cynic! I know the games people play, and I merely prefer to play them by my own rules. I set them down squarely first. And if I'm hard —" she shrugged, but straightened in her seat, her chin tilting a shade, her eyes glittering like blue crystals in the night — "it's because I have to be."

"Lost cause!" Jim muttered, pecking her forehead with a brotherly kiss before pulling his torso from the car. "Have a nice weekend. Give the kids a kiss for me, and I'll see you on Monday."

"Thanks, Jim," Sloan replied, twisting her key in the ignition. "Have a nice weekend yourself!"

Waving, she pulled out of the parking lot and onto the highway, breathing deeply of the crisp air. It was a beautiful night — the type that made her happy she had left Boston after Terry's death and returned home to Gettysburg. Stars dotted the sky like a spray of glittering rhinestones against a sea of black velvet. She passed the gently rolling landscape of the national park and smiled to herself wryly. It was the type of night when lovers should stroll together across fields of green in the tingling, crisp coolness.

But, she wondered briefly, would she ever really love again? Sloan hadn't lied to Jim. She had dated. Nice men, good-looking men, men she had even found attractive, at first . . . she had kissed them, felt their arms around her.

But remained absolutely untouched inside. Jim was the only person she saw steadily, and that was because he was a friend. He never pressured her.

Sometimes she felt as if her heart had frozen solid. She was hard, she was cold, she was cynical. She had to be a dead set realist. There were times when she still hurt too much, but she had to shelve loneliness and pain. Terry was dead. Point-blank. Fact. She had managed a life for herself, a fairly good one. She liked people, she saw people, she looked forward to the future. To a time when she could leave the survival pay of the college and work for a professional dance troupe again. Hire some help . . .

"What am I worrying about?" she asked herself impatiently as she drove up to her own house. She glanced at the pretty white building with the green trim with pride. She had purchased it herself, a great deal that her brother-in-law had found for her. She had made a good down payment, and now she only had the mortgage and taxes . . . and damn! A payment was due.

Sighing, Sloan decided to deal with that problem later. She walked briskly to her door and started to use her key, then thought better of the idea. Cassie startled easily. Better to knock than to scare her sister half out of her wits.

"Hi, kid!" Cassie greeted her, opening the door. "How was your night?"

Sloan shrugged as she tossed her purse onto a chair and bent in the doorway to slip off the straps of her heeled sandals and nudge them beneath the same chair. "Nice. The usual. Jim is a dear." She smiled at her older sister with resignation. "I do enjoy the evening out. Jim may not be exciting — but he is adult companionship!"

"I've got a pot of tea on," Cassie said. "Want some?"

"Naturally." Sloan laughed, following her pretty, slender sister into the kitchen. The women, only two years apart, were best friends. They shared the same tall, graceful build, but there the similarities of their appearances ended. Cassie had huge, saucer brown eyes and hair so light as to be platinum. At thirty-one, she was still looked at and asked for identification when she ordered a drink.

"Any problems?" Sloan asked as she accepted a mug of tea and curled her legs into a chair at the sunny yellow kitchen table.

"Not a one," Cassie replied, leaning her elbows on the table. "Jamie and Laura crawled into bed right after their super-hero program. And the baby, well, he's always an angel. He was sound asleep at seven."

Sloan warmed her face comfortably with the steam from her cup. "They know better than to mess with their aunt!" She chuckled. "Anything else new?"

Cassie hesitated, and Sloan watched her sister's beautiful brown eyes, puzzled. "What is it?"

"A man called for you, a Mr. Jordan."

"And?" Sloan prompted her sister casually, then held her breath as she waited for her answer. Mr. Jordan was with a professional dance company in Philadelphia.

"He said the job was yours," Cassie told her with troubled eyes. Then Sloan began to understand her hesitance.

"The salary?" she asked, holding her features in composure.

Cassie named a figure, and Sloan's heart

sank. She couldn't accept the job. She sighed as she realized she would probably be with the college dance department for years to come — she couldn't afford to quit. Not that she didn't like her job; she did. It was just that she so dearly longed to dance professionally again!

"Well then," Sloan said briskly with a forced smile. "That's that, I guess."

Cassie looked as if she were about to cry. "If only you hadn't had so many children!" she exclaimed miserably. Then she hastily added, "Oh, Sloan! I didn't mean that. I love the kids. But it's so hard for you alone."

"Well," Sloan said wryly, curling her lips a shade so that Cassie would know her words had been understood. "When Terry and I planned the children, we didn't intend that one of us would be raising them alone."

Terry had been a dreamer, and she had dreamed right along with him. They seemed perfectly mated, a dancer and an artist. In their first years they had struggled. Then, while Terry had been making his name as a painter, Sloan had gotten a terrific job with an ensemble in Boston. Luck followed the dreamers. When Sloan became pregnant with Jamie, Terry's oils caught on with the flurry of a storm. They lived happily. Terry was established; Sloan was able to combine

22

her professional dancing with motherhood. They planned Laura and the baby, Terence, for his father.

But Terry didn't live to see his namesake. He was killed when his flight home from Knoxville in a friend's small Cessna failed to clear the Blue Ridge Mountains. It took searchers three weeks to find his body, and when they did, Sloan was in the hospital, in labor two months early due to shock.

Dreamers never think to buy life insurance, and artists have no benefits. Sloan was snapped out of her grief by desperation — she had to support herself and her family. The baby, so premature, ate up any savings as he clung to life in his incubator. Terry's last pieces drew large sums as their value increased, ironically, with his death, but even that money did little but help Sloan return home to Gettysburg where her only comfort, Cassie, awaited.

Sloan buried the young dreamer she had been along with Terry's mutilated remains. In the first year she had mourned her happy-go-lucky husband with a yearning sickness that left her awake long nights in her lonely bed. She had gone through all the normal courses of grief, including anger. How could he have died and left her like he did? Resignation and bitter sadness followed her anger, and now she lived day to day, finding happiness in simple things. But she *had* closed in. The vivacious and beautiful woman whom people met was a cloak that concealed her true personality. She had toughened, and reality and necessity were the codes she lived by. She was friendly, sometimes flirtatious, but when anyone looked beyond those bounds, he would find a door slammed immediately in his face.

"Lord, I almost forgot to tell you!" Cassie exclaimed suddenly, sensing her sister's depression and trying to cheerfully dispel her gloom. "Guess who is in Gettysburg?"

Sloan chuckled. "You've got me. Who?"

"Wesley Adams."

"Who?" Sloan frowned her puzzlement. The name was vaguely familiar, but she couldn't picture a face.

"Wesley Adams! The quiet quarterback, remember? He's a couple of years older than I am, but the whole town knew him. He graduated from Penn State after high school, then went on to play professional ball. About four years ago he retired because of a knee injury and disappeared from public view." Cassie gave Sloan a wistful smile as she curled a strand of blond hair around her fingers. "I was secretly in love with him for years! And he asked *you* out! I think it was the one time in my life I absolutely hated you!"

Sloan frowned again. "I went out with Wes Adams?"

Cassie groaned with exasperation and threw her hands in the air. "She doesn't even remember! Yes, you went out with Wes Adams. He had just finished at Penn State, and you were eighteen, about to leave for Boston and your first year as a Fine Arts major. It was the summer before you met Terry. I set up the date — by accident, I assure you!"

Sloan laughed along with her sister. Cassie could easily talk about her memories; she was married to one of the most marvelous men in the world. George Harrington loved his wife and extended that love to encompass his sister-in-law. It was George who insisted he care for his own two boys on Friday nights so that Cassie could allow Sloan her evening out.

"I remember him now," Sloan said, wrinkling her nose slightly. "He reminded me of Clark Kent. Beautiful body, face enough to kill. But quiet! And studious! Our date was a disaster."

"Hmmph!" Cassie sniffed. "He was simply bright as all hell. And you, young lady, your head was permanently twisted in the clouds. You didn't like anyone who wasn't a Fine Arts major!"

Sloan quirked her brows indifferently. "Maybe. I was eleven years younger then than I am now. We all change." She rubbed sore feet. "Brother! I feel like my soles are toe-to-heel blisters. I must have been spinning half the day!"

"You're losing your appreciation for your art," Cassie warned with teasing consolation. "I seem to remember a comment you made once as a kid that you 'could dance forever and forever, into eternity!' "

"There's a slim chance that I did make such a comment," Sloan admitted dryly. "But if so, I must have been a good twenty years younger than I am now — and twenty times as idealistic?"

The ringing of the doorbell interrupted their idle chatter. "Gee . . . George already," Sloan mused.

"No . . ." Cassie was blushing and flustered. "I forgot to tell you . . . well, actually, you changed the subject before I got a chance." She was talking hurriedly as the bell continued to chime. "It's Wes Adams. I told you I saw him today and he asked me about you and I told him and . . ." She raised her hands helplessly. "I asked him over."

Sloan's mouth dropped with dismay. "To my house?"

"Don't be angry!" Cassie begged in a whisper. "He and George are old friends too. I thought we could all chat awhile. In fact, I even broke down and asked my mother-in-law to break up her beauty sleep and go watch the boys so that George and I could both stay out. And you know how the old battle-axe needs that beauty rest!"

"Cassie!" Sloan wailed.

"Oh, Sloan! What do you want me to do? I know that that's Wes at the door." Cassie bit her lip as she watched her sister. "Damn it, Sloan! Give the man a chance. He's a better prospect than anyone else around here. This is a small town. And" — she grinned mischievously as she rounded the kitchen corner to answer the clanging of the bell — "he's absolutely loaded! He moved to Kentucky when he retired and bought a Thoroughbred farm. He breeds racehorses."

"Terrific!" Sloan mumbled as she trailed after her sister. "He was dull to begin with, and now he's a farmer in Kentucky."

"He's not a farmer, he —"

"I know, I know. He raises Thoroughbreds. It's all the same to me."

"Put your shoes back on!" Cassie hissed.

Sloan grimaced painfully and slipped

back into her heels after diving beneath the chair to retrieve them. "Only for you, sister dearest!" she teased. "But give up on your matchmaking," she added in a low and serious tone. "I'm a twenty-nine-year-old widow with three children. I am too far-gone for romance!"

"Hush!" Cassie narrowed her brows, ran a hand over her smooth blond hair, and threw open the front door. "Wes!" she exclaimed happily in greeting. "I'm so glad you could make it!"

Wesley Adams returned her greeting with a warm smile and a friendly kiss on the cheek. "Thanks for inviting me, Cassie." He turned sea-green eyes to Sloan. "Sloan. How are you?"

"Good, thank you, Wesley." She accepted the hand he offered her and shook it briefly. "Come in. Sit down. *Cassie*" — she smiled pointedly to her sister — "will be happy to get you a drink."

Cassie shot Sloan a quick, murderous glare behind their visitor's back. "What can I get you, Wes?" she inquired extra sweetly, attempting to atone for Sloan's ill-concealed lack of hospitality. Her grin became impish. "You and *Sloan* can have a seat, and I'll play cocktail waitress."

"Terrific, thank you," Wesley said

smoothly. "I'd love a bourbon, if it's in the house supply."

"Certainly," Cassie murmured. "Sloan — a scotch?"

"A double — please." Sloan returned her sister's grin through clenched teeth as she politely took a seat beside Wesley Adams. He was still, she noted apathetically, a strikingly handsome man, probably more so with age. His shock of wavy hair, so dark as to be almost jet black, created an air of intrigue as it dipped rakishly in a natural wave over a brow. Faint lines etched his probing, intuitive eyes, lines which increased when he smiled with full lips. His face was bronzed and rugged; despite his navy suit and crisply pressed powder-blue shirt, he carried the definite air of an outdoorsman, an air which fit in well with his broad, powerful-looking shoulders and imposing height.

"I was very sorry to hear about your husband, Sloan," he said softly, sincere compassion in the sea-green eyes that met hers easily.

"Thank you." His unpatronizing sympathy touched a chord in her heart she had thought long since dead.

"I'm sorry again. Maybe I shouldn't have said anything."

"No, no, it's all right." She grudgingly gave him a faint smile. "Terry has been dead for two years. I assure you, I don't become hysterical at the mention of his name."

"You've changed," he remarked oddly.

"Have I?" Her smile became ironic. "I didn't realize you had known me well enough to judge such a thing."

The friendly smile he had been wearing remained glued to his face, but Sloan saw his facial muscles tighten as the warm spark in his eyes went cold. She winced imperceptibly at her own behavior. There was no need for her to be so uncivil.

Wesley Adams shrugged as he withdrew a pack of cigarettes from his vest pocket. He lit a cigarette, returned the pack to his pocket, and exhaled a long plume of smoke. His eyes were still on her, speculative and cold. Absurdly, she shuddered. Low-keyed and polite as he was, she had the strange feeling he could be dangerous if crossed.

"I didn't know you very well," he said casually, "but I do know that you never used to be out-and-out rude."

Sloan straightened as if she had been slapped. Of all the nerve! What a comment to make in her house! She drew breath for a caustic reply but snapped her mouth shut as Cassie gracefully sailed in from the kitchen

30

with a tray of drinks.

"Wes," Cassie said as she placed the tray on the mahogany coffee table. "That's your bourbon on the left. Sloan, scotch in the middle."

Sloan fell silent as Wes and Cassie began to converse with a pleasant camaraderie. Moments later, George put in his appearance, and after kissing his wife and sister-in-law, he accepted the Wild Turkey and soda his wife had precipitously prepared and assured her the boys were safe in bed and his mother happily ensconced before the television set enjoying an oldie about a monster that was threatening to eat New York. He, too, readily joined in the light banter, and the talk turned to football. Sloan allowed her mind to wander.

She admitted to herself that she had been rude and wondered why. Wes Adams meant nothing to her, yet he disturbed her. She had the strange feeling that he saw more with those unusual oceanic eyes than most people. He watched her as if she were an open book and he could read her every weakness.

Ridiculous. There were no weaknesses. Not anymore. She had learned to rely on Sloan Tallett and on no one else. She didn't know, not in her conscious mind, that the very goodness of her marriage now blocked an open heart. Terry had loved her; Terry had been wonderful. Terry had left her in the terrible mess she was in now. If someone had realized what lay in the uncharted recesses of her heart, they might have pointed out to her that she was blaming love for pain; blaming Terry for his own death as desertion. And if she could see, her eyes would widen and she would wince with horror at the reasoning that had left her as cold and as hard as steel. But she didn't see, and so she stiffened and went on.

And Wes Adams, the all but forgotten intruder who sat in her living room as if he belonged, was ruining the well-structured format of her life with his simple presence and cool words. It didn't matter, she told herself. He would be gone soon. And so would the inane feeling he gave her that she was losing control in some unclear way. She was always in control of any situation.

"And of course Sloan always joins in too," George was saying, his kindly gray eyes on her. He winked. "She's the high point of the summer!"

They were all looking at her now, and she flushed guiltily. "I'm sorry, George. I'm afraid I wandered. What do I join in to make this high point of the summer?"

"The school's annual summer dance!" Cassie hopped in impatiently. "Wes said he'd love to see you in a performance, and we told him he came at just the right time!"

"Oh," Sloan murmured, annoyed to feel herself blushing again as she met Wes's unfathomable, soul-piercing stare. What was the matter with her, she wondered impatiently. For the sake of the dance department she should be pushing the performance — glad of anyone who purchased a ticket and helped fill the immense auditorium. And by her own volition or not, Wes was a guest in her own home. A little cordiality wouldn't hurt. She slowly smiled and found it wasn't difficult at all when Wes curved his lips in return. "Our summer dance is quite a show," she told him, her enthusiasm growing. "We have some wonderful students."

He laughed easily. "I'll be looking at the teacher."

Absurd, but she felt herself blushing again, only this time the feeling wasn't uncomfortable. "What are you doing back in Gettysburg, Wes?" she asked, anxious to change the topic of conversation to anything other than herself.

"Business," he replied with a grimace. "And, of course, a little pleasure. This will always be home in a way. Mainly, I'm here on a buying trip — there's a man on the outskirts of the city who I do a lot of buying from. He has a knack with up-and-coming Thoroughbreds." Once again, Sloan was treated to a slow, subtly alluring smile. "At the moment," he continued, "I can honestly say I've never had a more pleasurable business trip."

Sloan managed not to blush again. With the hint of an enticing smile on her own lips, she inclined her head ever so slightly. Touché. He had learned to be a charmer when he chose.

From that point the night passed with surprising swiftness. Wesley, whom she had once found so boringly dull, proved to be an interesting speaker. His voice was a low tenor which still penetrated the room when he spoke, his words so appealingly phrased that Sloan was later shocked to realize she had listened to information on horses and football without once wandering from the conversation. It was after midnight when George finally looked at his watch and groaned that they had to leave.

"I'm sure New York has either been long consumed or saved by now," he said dryly, "and that my mother probably has her eyes propped open with toothpicks. How long will you be here, Wes?"

"A couple of weeks," Wesley replied, rising to shake his old friend's hand. "I'm sure we'll be able to get together again." He kissed Cassie lightly and took Sloan's hand. "Thank you, Sloan, for a pleasant evening."

"Thank you for coming," she parroted politely.

"Perhaps, if we have dinner one night, you'll join us."

Sloan wasn't sure if the invitation was sincere or not. She was being scrutinized by those uncanny eyes again, and the firm hand holding hers was mocking in its gentle but undeniable pressure. She smiled vaguely. "Yes, perhaps. But I have a problem with the children."

"I'm her only nighttime sitter," Cassie explained. "George's mother is too nervous to handle all five."

"That's no problem!" Wesley laughed, and for a moment his eyes seemed very warm and tender. "My housekeeper is with me, since I'm staying at my folks' home. They've been in Arizona for years now, so I assumed I'd need a bit of help with fixing up. Florence adores children. She'll be thrilled to watch them for us."

"I . . ." Sloan faltered helplessly. She didn't want to tell him that she didn't leave her children with just anyone — it would sound frightfully insulting.

But Wesley astutely sensed her dilemma. "I'll bring Florence by at your convenience so that you can meet her and she can meet the children. Then, if all goes well, we'll make a definite date for Saturday night, a week from tomorrow. Does that suit everyone?"

A little awed, Sloan nodded. It didn't just suit her, it sounded lovely. One of the reasons that she so seldom went out was the lack of available, trustworthy baby-sitters and a determination not to take advantage of her sister. She would also have trouble affording a regular sitter. "Loaded" Wesley was solving all her problems.

Wesley released her hand. George and Cassie kissed her good-night, and she was alone in her silent house with her sleeping children.

She was reflective that night as she showered and donned a light flannel gown, studying her face in the bathroom mirror. She winced at what she saw.

Although faint, tiny lines were forming around her eyes. Unlike Cassie, she certainly couldn't pass for eighteen. At least, she thought, giggling at her mirrored image, if she were to go prematurely gray, no one would notice. Her hair was already composed of too many colors.

Anyway, the hell with vanity. She was the mother of three. Still . . . her hand slid over her flat stomach. She was lucky. She had borne three children, yet come out of it without a scratch. Her figure was tighter than that of a teenager, her skin as smooth. Dancing, she told herself wryly. Her passion had kept her in shape.

But what difference did it make. There was no longer a man in her bedroom to tell her she was beautiful, to tell her what he loved about her. . . . No one to try to please. . . .

Sloan snapped out the light and peeked in on six-year-old Jamie, four-year-old Laura, and two-year-old "baby" Terry. They all slept soundly, their even breathing peaceful. Unable to resist, she tenderly kissed each little forehead. They were beautiful children, plump and healthy. Again, she reminded herself that she was lucky, and that she should be grateful and fulfilled.

I am fulfilled! she told herself sternly. There is nothing more I need than their love.

But she didn't sleep well that night. She was plagued by dreams of worry and emptiness.

Sloan pressed her hand over the mouthpiece of the telephone. "Jamie!" she wailed. "Quit torturing your sister! Give her back her doll! And hush up for five minutes!"

Jamie pursed his little lips, shot his mother a baleful glance, and returned his sister's doll. With a sigh, Sloan returned to her conversation.

"I'm sorry about the payment, Mrs. White, it must have been an oversight. I'll put it in the mail immediately. Please don't turn off the electricity!"

The woman on the other end spat off a few epitaphs about people who didn't pay bills on time and finally agreed to give her four days to have the payment in. Sloan hung up the receiver and rested her head tiredly on the phone.

"Mommy?" A tiny hand tugged on her sleeve, and she opened her eyes. Jamie — her devil, her love. "Mommy, I love you."

She picked him up and hugged him. "I love you, too, sweetheart. Now run along and see what your brother is doing."

She set him down and rubbed a hand across her forehead. No wonder she was getting wrinkles. She was always frowning.

"Mommy!" It was Jamie again. "Terry is putting the laundry in the toilet!"

"Eeeeeek!" Sloan screamed, racing into the bathroom. Lord, what next? She unstuffed the toilet and washed the baby, who gurgled happily with pleasure and lisped a few words. Then she returned to the kitchen to morosely sip her coffee, slumped into a chair.

"The morning," she told herself aloud, "is not going well at all."

Her mind, for no explicable reason, turned to Wesley Adams. He was a handsome man, polite and gracious. She unconsciously moved a hand over her face. He was attracted to her; she knew it intuitively. And he *was rich*. Wheels began to turn in her mind.

She sprang to her feet and raced back into the bathroom to anxiously study her reflection again. She smoothed the worried frown from her brow and smiled brightly. That was better. Much better. Maybe Jim's ideas for her future weren't quite so bad. . . .

She continued to stare at herself unseeingly for several seconds, oblivious to the playful ramblings of the children.

"I don't love him, I don't really like him. I hardly even know him!" she told the face that was forming before her, the face that had a bewitching but frighteningly predatory cast.

The children . . . I have to think of the children . . . and I'm so dreadfully tired of dealing with it all!

The face wasn't really predatory, she assured herself. Conniving, maybe, devious, yes perhaps . . . and hard. But not *predatory!* She swallowed, wincing, ashamed of her thoughts.

Sloan closed her eyes and turned away from the mirror, burying all sense of shame with purpose and determination as she did so. Like a marionette she jerked back to the phone and dialed her sister's number.

She chatted idly for a few minutes, then casually brought up the subject on her mind.

"What do you really know about Wesley Adams?" she asked.

Cassie rushed on with enthusiasm. Wes was wonderful. He had led his team to victory in the Super Bowl. He donated to charities all over the country. He had a beautiful spread in Kentucky where he raised his horses and held a summer camp for deprived children every year. . . .

"Does he really have that much money?" Sloan queried innocently, thankful that her sister couldn't see her face over the phone.

"Tons of it!" Cassie laughed. "His salary was unbelievable, and he seems to have the

Midas touch with investments. Everything he touches turns to gold, silver, and green. They had a big write-up on him in *Fortune* magazine when he left pro ball a few years ago. . . ."

Cassie had more to say, but Sloan was no longer listening. A slow buzzing was seeping coldly through her. She couldn't allow herself to think; she couldn't afford to moralize.

"Sloan?"

"I'm here, Cass."

"So — you've decided you like him after all! I knew you would. He's such a super guy! And he's interested in you. Half the women in this country would sell their souls to be in your place!"

"Yes, Cass." Sloan held her breath for a minute. She wasn't much of a liar, and she had never lied to Cassie in her life. Suddenly she felt hot, dizzy, and nervous — what she was planning was preposterous. She might have joked, but the idea of actually doing it had never occurred to her. Until now. And it had hit her with a jolt. It would be wrong; she couldn't . . .

But the last two years of her life flashed through her mind in a split second — a tumult of events that was dark and sobering. Terry's disappearance, the baby's premature birth, her own long haul back to health, having to quit the Fife Dance Company, moving back to Gettysburg and teaching at a salary that was more than she had made with Fife but still barely allowed her to make ends meet. "Yes, Cassie," Sloan repeated. "I think I like Wes very much now. I'm looking forward to our dinner."

"Sloan! I'm so glad! It's obvious that he still has some kind of a thing for you. . . ."

Cassie went on talking, but Sloan heard little of what she had to say. Somehow, she made all the right responses.

". . . fate and a little time . . ."

"Pardon?" Sloan inquired. Her mind had wandered a little too far.

Cassie sighed. "I said, 'who knows? With fate and a little time . . . ?' "

"Yeah," Sloan murmured. "I'd better get going, Cass. I have to go see what the little darlings are up to."

"Go!" Cassie chuckled. "I am so glad that you like him! Oh, well! Bye!"

"Bye. . . ." Sloan murmured faintly. She pulled the receiver slowly from her ear and sank into a chair, feeling light-headed. She did not replace the phone correctly, and a dull hum sounded to her ears.

Fate and time. She intended to give both more than a little push.

"God, I hope that I do like him!" she

whispered fervently to herself. She rose, a puppet again, and very meticulously adjusted the phone, cutting off the hum. Her plan took substance, and she spoke it aloud.

"I'm going to marry him."

Her voice was light, toneless, but the grim edge of determination rang clearly through.

# CHAPTER TWO

She hadn't actually done anything, but with her plan set in her mind, she felt the first pangs of guilt.

Rationalizing was in order. She put the baby and Laura down for their naps, supplied Jamie with pails and shovels for his sandbox, and moved into the back of the house, her studio.

The studio had been the one extravagant concession she had allowed herself to retain her art. The floor was an expensive wood to save wear on her feet and knees. A heavy metal exercise bar stretched the length of the left side, backed by a study mirror which covered the height and breadth of the wall. The right side of the room held huge bay windows which opened on the lawn, allowing her to work while watching the children at play. To the rear lay her stereo system, a good, complex one purchased when Terry had sold an elaborate set of landscapes.

When teaching, Sloan covered dance from classic form to aerobics. But to her the base for all dance was ballet, and when she engaged in her rigid workouts, it was to ballet exercises that she turned. Between stretches, pliés, and relevés, she came to terms with herself.

She planned to marry a stranger, a man she didn't love. It wasn't because she craved riches for herself, but because she would be able to provide a *decent* life for herself and her children.

And she swore she would never hurt Wesley Adams. She would never love again, she was sure, but Wesley would never know it. She would be everything he could possibly desire in a wife.

Her mind began to race with turmoil. How could she even think about doing a thing as despicable as marrying a man for his money? Marriage meant living with a man, sharing his life, sleeping in his bed. . . . A sick feeling stabbed her stomach. She changed the Bach on the stereo to a modern piece by a hard rock group and whirled about the room in a series of furious pirouettes and entrechats, hoping to exhaust her mind through strenuous dance. Sweat beaded on her brow, but it was as much from her thoughts as from her leaping jetés.

For a mother of three, she was painfully naive. Most of her friends had had one or two serious affairs before settling into marriage. Several were divorced and involved in new affairs, one after the other.

But for her, there had been only Terry. They had met when both were eighteen, married while still in school before either was twenty. It was all planned. A little over three years later they had their first child, Jamie. And in her years of marriage she had learned what intimacy between a man and woman truly meant. It meant giving oneself completely, trusting, opening up to vulnerability, accepting and loving — a part of a total commitment.

How could anyone even contemplate such a thing with a stranger?

She fell to the floor in a perfect split and stretched her nose to her knee. Don't be absurd! she snapped silently to herself. Sex was just a normal body function. Plenty of women she knew could easily sleep with any attractive male body. She closed her eyes, pushing such thoughts to the back of her mind. She would deal with her problems as she came to them. A little chuckle escaped her lips as she switched legs and her dark head bounced down to the other knee. *She* was planning a marriage. Maybe she wouldn't get to first base with Wesley Adams. According to Cassie, he could have his pick of females. Why should he *marry* her? Even if he was attracted to her. She was a twenty-nine-year-old widow with three children. He could probably have any number of bright, sweet young things — women who demanded no commitment and had no responsibilities to tie them down.

And then . . . Another thought nagged her. What if Wesley didn't get along with the children? She would never marry anyone, madly in love or not, unless he cared for the children and they for him.

Life, she decided with a wry grin, was a bitch.

But it could be so much better if she could only marry a kind, pliable man like Wesley Adams. She wouldn't always be worried about having to make a buck. She would be a good and true wife, but she would also be free to go her own way, to play with her children, to dance as she longed.

At that moment she closed her mind to right and wrong. Her heart hardened, not callously, but desperately. The dream of a good life was too sweet to allow for sentiment. She would use every one of her feminine wiles in the pursuit of Wesley Adams.

And there was no time to lose. He only planned to be in Gettysburg for two weeks.

"Mommy!"

Jamie's voice, screaming over the stereo, jolted her from her reflections. Her head jerked up guiltily, and she looked to her son in the studio door and then gasped with dismay.

Jamie was standing with the man who had so completely filled her thoughts, Wesley Adams. The man she had planned to captivate and sweep off his feet. And here she was, no makeup, sweat-streaked hair glued to her forehead, clad in a black leotard that had long since faded.

"Wesley!" she croaked, scrambling to her feet and unconsciously smoothing back a stray tendril of hair. Then she turned to her son with reproach. "Jamie, I told you never to answer the door! You must always get me."

"It wasn't the boy's fault," Wesley Adams explained with a crooked grin. His eyes were friendly, laughing, almost matching the knit, forest-green shirt that outlined his broad chest and well-muscled biceps. It wasn't difficult to return his grin.

"I rang," Wesley continued, "but no one came to the door. I heard the stereo, so I walked around back and found your son."

He tousled Jamie's light brown curls and hoisted the boy into his arms. "I convinced him I was a legitimate friend."

"Oh . . ." Sloan stammered weakly. This second meeting wasn't working out at all as she had planned. "I'm sorry I'm such a mess . . . I need a shower. . . . I — I wasn't expecting you this morning!"

He laughed easily, and she marveled at what a comfortable man he was. "I think you look stunning." His eyes roamed unabashedly over the trim but enticing figure so vividly displayed by the tight leotard. Yet his gaze held nothing licentious; it was one of teasing but respectful admiration. Foolishly, Sloan found herself blushing.

"Well, er, can I get you something?" she asked, laughing a bit nervously as she walked to the stereo to carefully lift the needle. "A cool drink? I have iced tea, lemonade, and oh, I think a few beers —"

"Run and take your shower, first," Wesley suggested, smiling at Jamie. "Then I'd love to have a glass of tea with you."

"Thanks," she smiled wryly. "But I can't. The baby should be waking up any minute."

"I'm the proud uncle of four nieces and six nephews," he told her. "If your little one wakes, I'm sure I'll be able to handle him."

"No!" Sloan protested. "I can't have you

49

watching my children —"

"Sure you can."

Sloan smiled uneasily. That lopsided grin of his could be most endearing and, and unnerving! He really was an attractive and . . . what? . . . man. Vital. The word sprang to her mind, followed by one even more disturbing — sexy. He may have retired from pro ball, but his sturdy structure and lithe movements proved him to be every inch an athlete.

"All right," Sloan murmured, confused by her jittery reaction to him. *I'm* the one out to entice him! she reminded herself. "Thanks. I'll just hop in and out. I'll hurry."

"Take your time, I'll be fine."

She smiled faintly as she sidled by him, warned Jamie to be good, and hurried into the shower. Once there, she did take more time than she had intended. She scrubbed her skin pink and worked her hair into a rich lather with scented shampoo. It wouldn't dry, she realized as she fluffed it with a towel, but clean wet was better than sweaty wet! She splashed herself with a light daytime cologne that smelled of fresh fields and applied a touch of low-keyed makeup. Satisfied with the results, she slipped into a pair of hip-hugging jeans and a cool halter top. Although the nights were cool, the Pennsylvania summers could be murder in the day.

She emerged from the bathroom feeling much more confident. The role of femme fatale was played more easily in the right costume. Affecting a brilliant smile, she moved into the living room with a calculated walk.

The children were all awake, all ensconced on Wesley's lap as he sat on the floor with them, embellishing a worn book of fairy tales. A painful little tug pulled at her heart as she watched the scene.

Wesley hadn't lied; he was a natural with children. Even two-year-old Terry sat with wide eyes glued on the storyteller's face.

Sloan forget all about her bewitching smile and swinging walk as she paused in the hallway, an erratic pulse beating through her veins. *He liked the children. He hadn't even let a day go by without coming to see her. The more she saw of him, the more she liked.*

The tale of Cinderella, told in his deep, compelling voice, came to an end with the prince and princess living happily ever after. Laura jumped to her feet, demanding another story.

"Not now, my pet," Sloan said softly, coming to scoop her daughter into her arms with a laugh. Laura's eyes were huge and blue like her own, and they snapped with outrage, causing Sloan and Wesley both to chuckle.

"Mommy!" Laura began her protest. "Go back to the bathroom."

"Hey, young lady!" Sloan chastised her. "Don't you talk to me like that."

"Remember our promise!" Wesley intercepted quickly, sneaking a wink which encompassed the three children.

"Pizza!" Jamie happily expounded to his mother. He never could keep a secret.

"If it's all right with your mother," Wesley said sternly. "And if you behave for the rest of the afternoon." He glanced at Sloan apologetically. "I hope you'll forgive a bit of bribery."

Sloan bit back a chuckle and sank gracefully to the floor beside them. "The best of us stoop to it now and then. Kids," she said, praying they chose to obey without argument, "go on into the playroom for a while now." She glanced at Wesley with raised "you asked for it" brows. "Mr. Adams will read you another story later."

Surprisingly, the children grudgingly wandered toward the playroom, baleful glances at their mother their only sign of pique. Sloan waited until they had cleared the room to look to Wesley, breathing deeply as she reminded herself she must move with all speed.

"Thank you," she murmured, unnerved to find it difficult to meet his frank, unwavering green gaze. "That was kind of you."

"I told you. I like kids."

Sloan didn't try to look at him again. Running a slender hand along the shag of the rug, she continued, "I want to apologize for last night. You were right. I was being rude and I'm . . . I'm sorry."

He laughed, the slow easy laugh she was coming to like so much. "You're totally forgiven. I did rather barge in after a long day. But I'll extract a payment if I may. I supply the dinner, but I get to stay for it. How's that?"

"All payments should be so amiable!" She crossed one foot over the other and rose. The light, masculinely pleasant scent of his after-shave was drifting to her nostrils; she was becoming too fascinated by the display of his long rugged fingers as they lay casually upon a muscled thigh. "Come on, I'll get our tea."

Wesley proved to be a perfect guest. He didn't seem to mind in the least that the afternoon was spent checking on two-year-old Terry, nor was he adverse to wiping tomato sauce from little faces after the pizza arrived. When bedtime rolled around, he insisted on giving the boys their bath, after which he expertly taped a plastic overnight diaper on newly potty-trained Terry. True to his word, he read the children another story and tucked them into bed. They barely remembered to kiss their mother, and Sloan wondered with amusement whether to be offended or pleased.

She perked coffee while she waited for Wesley to finish with the children, arranging a tray anxiously to bring to the living room table for a more relaxed setting. Where did she go from here? Things were going too well. Wesley, by appearing at her door without warning, had thrown her completely off course. What was it he was after? She couldn't play too hard to get, or he might disappear for good. Yet she couldn't be an easy conquest. Marriage was her game, nothing else, or all was wasted.

Wesley sauntered into the kitchen as she placed a ring of crackers around small squares of cheddar and Muenster cheese. "They're quite a handful," he remarked with a long stretch. "You must be a veritable powerhouse of energy." He nonchalantly reached for a cracker and slice of cheese. "How do you do it all?"

Sloan cocked her head with a short, convincing laugh. It wouldn't do to let him know that she wasn't managing well with "doing it all." "They are actually pretty good kids," she said. "They go to a great day-care center when I work, and Cassie lets me out on Friday nights. It's not such a bad life and I . . ." Her voice broke off suddenly.

"What?" The sincere compassion in his eyes urged her to go on.

"I wouldn't trade a one of them for anything in the world," she said softly.

"I don't blame you." Wesley picked up the tray and preceded her to the living room. "Good coffee," he commented as he sat comfortably on the sofa. The crooked grin softened his rather severely chiseled features, blending the angles of his high cheekbones and square, rugged jaw. "Good coffee is a sign of a good woman, you know."

It was easy to laugh with him, and she needn't have worried about the evening. He made no move to touch her as they talked, and she again found him interesting as they discussed a number of subjects. He wasn't Terry, he didn't fill the air with imaginative views and vociferous dreams, but as the time passed by them, she slowly forgot to make comparisons.

"So tell me more about you," he said suddenly, disarming her with the question thrown casually into general conversation.

"There's nothing to tell," she said, fiddling with her empty coffee cup as he lit a cigarette. Remembering what she was up to, she batted murky lashes with a sweet smile. "You've spent the day here; you've seen it all."

"Why did you give up dancing?"

She feigned a cough. She certainly couldn't tell him her strained finances were the cause. "I haven't given it up. I teach now. As for going back and joining a company full time . . . I'd have to head for a larger city, and with the children small, I like the size of Gettysburg."

"You danced when your husband was alive." It wasn't a question, but a statement of fact. Sloan replied slowly, puzzled at his sure knowledge.

"Yes, when Terry was alive he could be with the children nights. He painted at home, and his work was doing very well —" She broke off swiftly, frightened that she had come so close to giving herself away. Falling into another radiant smile, she hastily turned back his question. "How did you know that I was dancing when Terry was alive?"

Tiny dimples appeared in Wesley's bronzed cheeks. "I saw you in Boston.

About seven years ago."

"Oh!" His revelation was startling. "What were you doing in Boston."

"Celebrating with friends. My team won the Super Bowl that year, and we were about crazy after the hectic season and grueling training." The dimples flashed again as he grimaced. "I think I fell in love that night. You were absolutely magnificent. Half the audience must have known from my shouting that you were a girl from my own town."

"Really?" Sloan laughed, but she eyed him nervously. He was teasing her, of course, flattering her. "Why didn't you come backstage?"

"Because I knew you were married."

"Oh." A silence hung heavily on the air between them. Sloan reached awkwardly for the tray to return it to the kitchen, but Wesley's hand came over hers. She started nervously and met his probing green gaze. His touch had felt like an electrical charge.

"Tell me about your husband," he said softly. "It's obvious that you loved him very much. I'd like to hear about him."

"Terry?" Sloan's eyes clouded to a misty blue. "Terry was a dreamer, a happy-go-lucky dreamer. He was a wonderful man; he loved the world. He was very talented and" — she couldn't lie about Terry — "yes, I

57

loved him very much."

"Do you have any of his work?"

"Only one piece," she said lamely. How could she explain that she'd had to sell the others? She couldn't. She'd have to spin another notch in her web of lies.

"Terry lost most of his paintings in the accident."

"I'd like to see the painting that you have."

"I'm afraid it's of me," Sloan said apologetically, rising. "It's in my bedroom." She turned to lead the way quickly, annoyed to find that she was blushing again.

The painting, she believed, was Terry's finest piece. He had caught her in a graceful pirouette, her hair spinning red and gold around her, her dress of sheer gauze fluttering in touchable folds. The painting seemed to live, the radiance of the dance immortalized for eternity in the vibrant blue exuberance of her eyes. No amount of poverty could ever bring her to sell the painting. It had been a special gift from Terry, a tangible link to the essence of what they both had been.

Wesley stood staring at the painting for a long time. "He was a very fine artist," he finally said. "A brilliant one." He turned to her suddenly. "I assume it's not for sale."

"No," Sloan said. Then she moistened very dry lips. It was time to take a shot in the dark. "No," she repeated with what she hoped was a sensuous smile. "I'm afraid the painting goes with me. You can't have one without the other."

"Oh?" His brows raised slightly, and there was a definite, mischievous glint in his eyes. "Well, I have already determined to have the one."

Time hung suspended, and static rippled the air as Sloan stared at him, not breathing, mesmerized. Who is seducing whom here? she wondered briefly.

Wesley broke the invisible bonds that stretched between them. "I've got to get out of here." He chuckled, glancing at his watch. "I've way overstayed my welcome." He glanced back to Sloan, his eyes light yet strangely guarded. "What do you do on Sundays?"

"Uh . . . laundry, usually," Sloan stammered, annoyed that she should give him such a humdrum reply, but not as quick as he to break the spell of the unnerving moment.

Wes grinned with lazy ease. "Could I twist your arm into doing something else?"

Sloan laughed sheepishly. "You could twist my arm easily, but I'm afraid I still can't go out. Cassie and George spend the day with his parents and —"

"And the children would need a sitter," Wes finished for her. "But they might as well meet Florence and get to know her early."

Not quite sure what he meant by such a comment, Sloan offered another weak protest. "Wesley, how can we just spring three children upon this lady? I'm sure she's busy with your house —"

"Florence would rather be busy with kids any day. And I promise you, she's a wonderfully unique person. She doesn't just tolerate little ones — she loves them."

Sloan lifted helpless hands. "What did you have in mind?"

"That, Mrs. Tallett, is a loaded question!" Wes warned teasingly. "If I answered you honestly, you'd throw me out." He was serious, bluntly, appraisingly so, but his winning grin took the sting out of the words. Even so, Sloan blushed. "Since I don't dare answer you honestly," he continued without apology, "what would you say to a picnic in the park?"

"A picnic sounds nice," Sloan mouthed automatically.

"Good," Wes said quickly, before she could think. "I'll be by tomorrow about ten with Florence. Is the time okay?"

"Fine. . . ." Sloan murmured, dazed. She was supposed to be the aggressor here, but so far she wasn't working very hard.

Wesley smiled and kissed her cheek lightly, as he had her sister's the previous evening. "Good night, Sloan." His long strides brought him quickly to the front door. "Thank you for a wonderful day."

"Thank you," Sloan called, but he was gone. Still dazed, she returned to the living room and picked up the coffee tray.

Everything was working out perfectly — to her benefit. Even in her moments of highest confidence, she had never imagined that Wes would make it so easy for her to set her little marriage trap. Instead of feeling wildly victorious, she was nervous as hell. As pleasant as Wes continued to be, there was a quality about him that was quietly powerful.

He had been a professional football player, she reminded herself. Such a sport bred a man who was innately domineering, physically fit . . . threatening with that primitive, almost untamed masculinity.

"What a ridiculous thought!" she chastised herself aloud. She was turning Wes into a charging tiger that might pounce in a moment of brute force. He was nothing like that. And she wasn't a member of an op-

61

posing defense to be tackled or plowed out of the way.

Still, there was something about him. She had sensed it that first night. Something that hadn't been there in his youth. A confidence and control that allowed him to be pleasant because he would have the strength to handle any situation that did get out of control with quick, ruthless ease.

She shivered suddenly, and the shivering brought her out of her mental wanderings. She realized she was still rinsing a well-rinsed cup. "I'm inventing things!" she whispered to herself. "Wes is the nice guy he appears to be. And he likes me. . . ."

But how did he "like" her? He was thirty-four, but he had never married. She was sure — simply from that virile masculinity that he exuded — that he had had a multitude of affairs. He was a sensual man — she was already keenly aware of his effortless magnetism. He was probably thinking of nothing more than an affair now.

"It can't be just an affair!" Sloan spoke aloud to herself again, her tone desperate. He had to marry her!

He wanted her. Even if her instincts had been faulty, he had come right out and said as much. Yet how badly did he want her? Enough to marry her?

A flash of heat washed over her from head to toe as she thought about the strange moment when they had stood together in her bedroom doorway. Admittedly, she had felt stirrings she hadn't experienced in over two years. Her senses had reeled more from his mere nearness than they had from any kiss by a would-be suitor.

Sloan dropped the saucer she had been holding into the dishwasher and crouched to the floor, circling her knees with her arms. She was attracted to Wesley, and the feeling was terrifying. She had to keep the upper hand; she had to be able to deny and demur all the time.

"And I will!" She fought the dizzy confusion that had assailed her like a forceful wind and stood, shaking herself. Lord! she told herself impatiently. I'm a twenty-nine-year-old widow! Not some naive half-wit! Not the type of sweet innocent to be led stupidly like a slaughtered lamb into a bed of seduction!

Semiconvinced, she straightened her shoulders unconsciously. She wasn't exactly an overly humble fool, either. She was aware of her assets — a dancer almost had to be. She knew how to play the games of flirtation and seduction herself. Granted, she had never set out to be the vamp before, but it was a role she could — and would — assume.

This was a game she was determined to win.

Sighing, she wiped the kitchen counter and slowly folded the dish towel. There was no way she was going to be happy and at ease until . . . until the game was over. Her mind was waging too many wars. It was wrong . . . she knew it was wrong to purposely set out to marry someone for money, no matter how she swore to herself to be a good wife. She should bow out of the game before it ever began. She couldn't begin to imagine what had possessed her in the first place to come up with such an idea.

But she had come up with it. And now it had become a dream . . . a dream of security that was so good she couldn't forget it, couldn't pretend that it had never existed.

Sloan bit into her bottom lip so hard as she walked into her bedroom to slip into her nightgown that she drew blood. There was no going back now. Wesley might not know that he was now engaged in the biggest game of his life, but he was. Another Super Bowl.

And this time, he was going to lose.

Sloan slipped between her sheets and turned off her bedside lamp. Even with her mind irrevocably made up, it was a long time before she slept. She tossed and turned and woke several times. She had been dreaming, but she couldn't quite put her finger on just what it was in her dreams that kept awakening her.

Finally, as the pale light of dawn crept slowly through the windows telling her that her fitful night was almost at an end, she realized what was bothering her.

She was no longer seeing Terry's thin, carefree face in her dreams. She was seeing Wesley's. The penetrating, oceanic green eyes. The pitch black hair with the wings of silver. The hard, angular, strong planes of his face. The rugged jawline. The full, sensual lips curving over perfect white teeth.

For the first time in two years she was actually dreaming of another face. Wesley's smiling face.

But a smiling face that was very disturbing. Because in her dreams the smile was cold. It didn't reach to eyes that were as sharply condemning as a jagged dagger of ice.

# CHAPTER THREE

Perversely, with the coming of light, Sloan found herself finally able to sleep. Waking fully to recognize her dreams had put them to rest. Wesley had been nothing other than charming to her, and, if he continued with his persistence, the next two weeks would prove to be enjoyable and exciting.

It seemed that her alarm went off as soon as she was deeply encircled in a comfortable sleep. Grudgingly Sloan rose — her usual scurry of morning activity was about to begin.

The children had to be bathed and dressed and fed, and then today she had herself to worry about. Most Sundays she didn't bother with makeup but simply scrubbed her face, tied back her hair, and threw on a pair of jeans. The laundry didn't care much what she looked like.

Today was different.

Today she very carefully applied just the right amount of makeup to enhance her own coloring while still appearing natural. She heated her curling wand to tighten the light waves of hair which escaped her ribbon to fall about her face in delicate tendrils. She hesitated long over her casual clothing before choosing a pair of flattering shorts and a cotton, kelly-green blouse with puff sleeves and sash closings which tied in front between the breasts.

As she had hoped and planned, the effect was perfect.

She looked young and carefree, as charming and natural as a wood nymph. No one would ever take her for a mature matron about to complete her third decade of living.

That dash of excitement she had been feeling gleamed brilliantly in the sapphire of her eyes. She laughed exultantly. "Careful, girl!" she warned herself. "Looking like a teenager doesn't mean you should be acting like one!"

She had stooped to tie her sneakers when the doorbell rang. Jamie — remembering his lesson of the previous day — called to her, "Door, Mom!"

"Thank you, Jamie," she told him, tweaking his cheek as she passed him. "That's going to be Wesley and his friend who is going to watch you. Please be good, Jamie!"

"Ahh . . . Mom!" Jamie declared indignantly. "I'm always good."

"Oh yeah?" Sloan raised a doubting brow to him but smiled. Jamie was good — old for his six years, a stout defender for his younger sister and brother. He had been young when he lost his father, and his world had turned around, but he was a sensitive child, like the father he lost, and he intuitively knew when things were going especially rough for his mother.

"I'm going to be a living doll!" he promised with wide eyes. Still smiling, Sloan opened the door. Wesley stood there in faded, tattered jeans and an old football jersey, his rich, dark hair gleaming like a raven's wing in the glare of the sun. A broad grin stretched across his face as he greeted her with sparkling eyes of appreciation.

"Good morning. Am I too early?"

"No . . . good morning." Why am I always stammering around him? Sloan wondered. She had seemed caught in the spell of his eyes again, frozen into forgetting who she was, where she was. . . .

"May we come in?"

"We?"

"Yes, I'm sorry. Florence —" Wes turned from the doorway, and Sloan saw a tiny, middle-aged woman who had previously

68

been hidden by Wesley's broad, sinewed frame. "Sloan, this is Florence Hendry. Florence, Sloan Tallett. And those little faces peeping around her knees are Jamie, Laura, and Terry."

Sloan smiled hesitantly, suddenly as shy as the children who withdrew their curious heads quickly. But the tiny woman had eyes as warm as the sun, and the smile she gave in return was full and heartening. "Sloan," she said softly, taking the slender, outstretched hand firmly, "what a pleasure. Wesley has spoken of nothing but you since we arrived." Her crinkled face dimpled. "I will admit, though, that I'm most anxious to meet the children."

Sloan stepped aside, realizing that her company was still standing in the doorway. "Mrs. Hendry, the pleasure is mine. Please, come in. Jamie, Laura, Terry — say hello to Mrs. Hendry. She'll be staying with you today —" Sloan bit lightly on her lower lip and glanced quickly from Wes — standing benignly amused in the background — to Florence. "Are you sure this isn't too much trouble for you? Opening a house must have you busy —"

"I have no schedules!" Florence laughed. "And please, call me Florence. I'm pleased to death to spend a day with your children. I

69

miss all the little ones at home."

Sloan couldn't prevent her startled glance from flying to Wesley's face. He read her unasked question and threw up hands in mock protest. "Not mine!" he laughed. "I told you I was riddled with nieces and nephews — four of whom live with me. I went into the Thoroughbred business with my brother."

"Oh," Sloan murmured, feeling a flush rise to her cheeks. "Well, uh, Florence, let me show you a bit of the house. The refrigerator is stacked with sandwich meat —"

"Which we won't need," Florence supplied cheerfully. "We're going to have our picnic here. Wes had them make us two baskets at the deli," she explained. "So you just tell me any special instructions."

"I really don't have any special instructions," Sloan murmured, leading Florence on a quick tour of the downstairs. "If you need anything, Jamie will help you. Their rooms are full of toys and books. . . ." Sloan grinned sheepishly as they returned to the living room. "I'm not sure what else I should tell you."

"We'll get along famously," Florence said with assurance.

Sloan was sure that they would. The little woman who had breezed into her life along with Wesley was like a fairy godmother. Mature, confident, cheerful. The type person who made you immediately feel as if everything was all right.

"Well . . ." Sloan murmured again, surprised and a little disoriented to see that the children had already lost their shyness. Jamie was having a very mature conversation with Wes, and Laura and Terry were looking at Florence with eager anticipation. "I'll just get my sunglasses . . ."

No one seemed to notice as she ran back into the kitchen and searched the ledge above the sink which was a catchall. She dug her glasses out of a pile of coupons and savings stamps, pausing for a breath of air.

She felt as if she were walking on clouds. It was actually Wes who had brought the magic into her life. He lifted a hand, went poof, and all her problems were solved. He thought of everything. Their day stretched brightly before them — free and clear.

Of course, her problems would all come back in the morning. But she was — all scheming aside — exhilarated by the idea of the picnic she was about to go on. She was anxious . . . eager . . .

"Sloan! What are you doing, having those sunglasses made?" Wesley's demand, called from the living room, rang with a teasing tolerance.

"Coming!" she called in return.

Sloan paused for a second as she entered the living room unnoticed. Florence, despite her rather severe, hawk-shaped nose and the ramrod posture of her tiny frame, was perched easily on the floor while she drew the children out, telling them about Kentucky and all the horses, ponies, and dogs and cats that lived on the farm. Wesley was beside her, allowing a giggling Jamie to climb upon his powerful shoulders.

"Mommy!" Jamie cried, seeing her at last. "Wesley is giving me a ride."

"So I see."

Wesley grinned up at her a little sheepishly. "All set?"

"All set."

"Okay, Jamie," Wes said, setting his small charge down. "We'll be back in a bit. Take care of Florence."

"I will," Jamie vowed gravely.

Sloan kissed each of her kids and followed Wes to the door. She glanced back to Florence and started to open her mouth.

"I'm fine!" Florence insisted before she could say anything. "You two get going and have a nice day."

"We are going," Wesley answered for her,

clamping a hand over Sloan's mouth, which brought a burst of laughter from the children. "Bye — and you all have a nice day too!"

Sloan was giggling as Wesley led her out to his car, a plush, comfortable Lincoln, with his hand still clamped over her face. He released her only to usher her inside. "You," he accused as the car leveled onto the highway, "are a very protective parent."

"I'm sorry —" Sloan began.

"Don't be sorry," Wes interrupted, his right hand momentarily squeezing hers before returning to the wheel. "I think it's a wonderful trait. If I ever have kids — which I hope to one day — I think I would be every bit as protective."

Sloan smiled a little uneasily. She wondered what he would think if he knew she was already planning on his having kids — three, ready-made. But she didn't spend much time brooding. Even the weather seemed to benignly assist her in her secret quest. The sun shone golden in the sky, and a gentle breeze stirred to keep the heat from becoming oppressive. The grass at the park had never seemed greener, the day more lustrously blue, the air more exhilarating.

"Shade or sun?" Wes asked after the Lincoln was parked. He handed Sloan a small cooler from the trunk as he grabbed the heftier food basket himself along with a wide blanket.

"Shade, I think," Sloan chose. "I'm out so little that I have to be careful not to burn."

Wes smiled noncommittally and led the way to a draping sycamore that provided a broad and gentle shelter. "Okay?"

"Perfect."

Sloan was overwhelmed by that strange shyness again as Wes competently spread out the blanket and adjusted the basket and cooler. Absurd sensation! she told herself with an inward shake. Some vamp I'm shaping up to be!

Determined not to behave like a gauche, tongue-tied girl, she sat leisurely on the blanket and started the conversation rolling herself. "You were right about your housekeeper. She's wonderful. Where did you find her?"

"I didn't." Wes grinned, half reclining beside her and opening the cooler to pull out a pair of semifrosted glasses and a bottle of Chablis. "Grab the glasses, will you? As to Florence" — he poured wine for them each — "she raised me. Her husband was killed in World War II, and she determined never to marry again, but she was crazy about kids, so she went to work for my mother.

When my folks decided to move to Arizona, they sent Florence after me. They were worried — a little belatedly, since I was thirty at the time — but they thought a bachelor football player might not take care of himself properly."

"Too much of a wild life, eh?" Sloan chuckled, sipping her wine and feeling relaxation steal over her.

"Not too wild," Wes replied. "Thirty in sports is middle-aged. As a dancer you must know that there's only so much you can do to a body and expect it to keep functioning properly."

"You must have quit shortly after," Sloan observed. She hesitated slightly, hoping she wasn't traveling into troubled waters. "Cassie mentioned you had a knee injury. Was it serious?"

Wes shrugged. "Ligaments," he replied casually. "I could have just sat out a season, but I'd had enough. I played for ten years. I wanted to get into something else while I was still young enough to give it everything that I had. Dave — my brother — had started with the horses on a small scale a few years before and so" — he lifted his shoulders and dropped them, turning lazy eyes to her as he took a sip of wine — "there's the whole story."

Sloan chuckled. "By what I hear from Cassie — she's one of your staunchest fans, you know — there's a lot more to the story than that."

He shrugged again and plunged into the picnic basket. "Nope. That's about it. A lot of monotony in between a few broken bones and sprained ankles."

"But you never married." The words were out before Sloan realized what she was saying. Prying a little was one thing — pushing too fast could get her into hot water.

"No, I never married." His glance was cool and fathomless. "What would you like to start with? We have all kinds of salads, fried chicken, fried shrimp and — I am good at this if I do say so myself — I have a honey dip for the chicken and a choice of tartar or cocktail sauce for the shrimp."

"I think I'll start with everything," Sloan murmured, a little uneasy since she had so openly pried and thinking it might be to her benefit to keep her mouth busy for a while with food. "I just realized I'm ravenous, and . . . you are very good at this!"

"Thank you." Wes dunked a shrimp into the plastic container of cocktail sauce and popped it into her mouth. He laughed at her surprised expression, and the unease she had been feeling slipped away.

They both talked as they ate, and they began to learn a great deal about one another. While she managed to draw information diplomatically from Wesley about his summer camp and the battering years of pro football, he managed to get her talking about Terry. It was strange that she could talk about her deceased husband with Wes, a man she was supposedly seducing, when she found it difficult to talk about Terry to anyone. But he seemed interested, genuinely sympathetic. He seemed to offer her strength . . . silly. It was simply the way he was built, and the character that the years had ingrained in his face. Next to such a man it was easy to feel that he could take away the cares of the world and set them upon his own broad shoulders.

It was later in the day, after a bottle of wine and a half of the feast he had provided had been consumed, that Sloan contentedly made an admission to herself.

She was happy. Honest-to-God happy. Wesley had made no passes at her, but she felt herself drawn to him, at ease with him, comfortably so. He sat beside her, his compelling green eyes laughed into hers, his strong hand brushed over hers often, naturally. And she could feel him, his heat, his suppressed strength, his handsome frame so close to hers that it almost made her dizzy.

No, it was the wine making her dizzy. No, it was Wesley. . . .

She blushed suddenly as they lay in lazy companionship, comfortably relaxed beneath the sycamore. She realized where her thoughts had been taking her.

She had been wondering what it would be like to be held in his arms . . . to feel his lips commanding hers . . . to lie beside him, flesh against flesh, and feel the mastery of his superb muscles. . . . It was more than a blush, and she was glad his astute green eyes were idly upon the sky instead of her. Crimson splashed its way through her body, heating her from head to toe. What's the matter with me? she demanded of herself. I'm not that sort of person!

But something else inside of her was crying out. *What* sort of a person. It had been so long . . . and she was a mature woman, a normal woman. It was only natural that she should feel the need for strong, masculine arms around her, revel in the faint and intoxicating aroma of after-shave and . . . and . . . simple *maleness.*

"Shall we?"

"What?" Startled, Sloan glanced at Wes.

He was no longer watching the sky; he was watching her.

"Sleeping on me, huh?" he teased, knowing full well her mind had wandered. "Nice. Real nice. I take the girl out and put her right to sleep! I said, 'Shall we take a walk?' "

"Oh — uh — yes, sure." She smiled quickly. "A walk sounds nice."

Wesley rose, moving with the agility that only an athlete could possess, and extended a hand to Sloan. She unwound her own legs and gracefully accepted his assistance up, her mind beginning to race.

Where was he leading her . . . ?

It was a public park, she told herself coldly. He wasn't leading her anywhere. But she began to feel a tinge of fear, and it had nothing to do with Wesley's far superior strength or what he might attempt to do.

She was afraid of herself. The touch of his hand on hers was warm, commanding . . . inviting. She wanted to accept that invitation; she wanted to feel more and more of him. . . .

Face it, she was attracted to him. Very attracted to him.

Which was a damned good thing! her mind hollered out even as she faced him with a smile on her lips and a guard carefully cast over her eyes. She was plotting to marry him, rationalizing the action by telling herself she was going to be a good wife. If she was going to be such a good wife, it was an awfully good thing she was going to be able to respond. . . .

"How about the trail?" Wes queried, pointing off into the trees. "I think it offers a little privacy."

"Wonderful. . . ." Sloan heard herself saying weakly. His arm was around her shoulder as they started off on the pine path and ambled into its delightful coolness. For a while they walked in companionable silence, speaking only occasionally in whispers as they pointed out the little gray squirrels that skittered in starts from tree to tree. Then they reached a small glen, hemmed in by the graceful fingers of pines, carpeted by beds of lush, green grass. Wesley sank down and pulled her beside him, face to face, half-prone on nature's chaise.

Sloan's nerves were as taut as piano wire. She was frightened; she was eager. Her pulses were racing in a crazy zigzag of yes and no while her heart pounded so loudly she was sure it must echo through the quiet of the surrounding forest. He was going to kiss her. She was no longer going to have to wonder about the feel of his corded arms because they were going to come around her. . . .

But they didn't, not right away. He smiled at her, an incredibly sensuous, lazy smile as he lay back in the earth's soft cushion of the glen and openly relished the simple pleasure of watching her, the sea of his eyes languorously moving from the delicate lines of her profile — hesitating at the enticing hint of firm breast displayed to such advantage by the knot of her blouse — to the angular plane of her hip and along the slender but dancer-shapely length of her long legs.

A bird chirped somewhere in the branches above them, but Sloan was barely aware of its cheerful cry. It was part of the hypnotism this man was exuding, part of the compelling aura that seemed to make an island of the glen, an isolated place of beauty where all that was real was the shelter of the friendly pines, the encouraging whisper of the breeze, the soft, earthy bed of green and brown, and — the dynamically handsome man who lay before her, emanating an undeniable virility.

He dropped the blade of grass he had been idly chewing and stretched a tanned finger to outline the softness of her lips. They trembled at his touch and parted, and the finger went on to rub gently the edge of her teeth as he watched, fascinated. A

81

shudder ripped through Sloan, one of such abject longing that it left her shocked by its vehemence and quivering in its wake. But still he didn't reach for her, but spoke instead, and his voice was part of the breeze, a whisper as compelling and hypnotic as his piercing sea-jade eyes.

"You're exquisite," he said. "Incredibly beautiful," and his eyes were still locked with hers; his finger still touched her lips. His head moved toward hers until it was just an inch away, and he murmured, "I want you to know that my intentions are entirely honorable."

"What?" Sloan mumbled, confused and deep within the spell of the moment. She knew she should be listening; she should be talking; she should be coyly denying his touch. But all her scheming seemed worlds away. There was something else at stake, but she couldn't remember what. A pulse was beating erratically through her system. Her veins felt as if they were composed of a silvery liquid which raced like mercury in response to the simple feel of his finger; her nerves were so vibrantly alive that she could feel every touch of the gentle breeze, every blade of grass that brushed her skin. Her whole body was crying out, silently pleading for the excruciating pleasure of the muscle-rippled bronzed arms which must surely take her into their demanding security soon.

And they finally did, like lightning. A powerful hand crushed her lithe softness to his lean hardness as he groaned. "I'm crazy about you," he murmured huskily. "I always have been. And you're more beautiful than ever . . ." He intended to say more, but the moist, inviting lips parted tantalizingly before him were too much. He kissed her, nibbling her lower lip, probing with tender but firm command until she moaned and fell entirely acquiescent to his seduction of her mouth. Then the kiss became wild and passionate, and everything was forgotten and unreal as she strained against him, a willing prisoner of the all-encompassing, delightfully sensual sensations he was arousing. His lips left hers to create a burning trail along the sensitive flesh of her neck and down to the partially exposed mounds of her breasts; the unhurried, assured exploration of his hands sought her intimately, discovering the lean muscles of a thigh, delighting in the slender slope of a hip, creating an inferno of yearning along the bare flesh of her midriff. His seeking moved upward so that he might cradle the lushness of her breasts, and she made no protest as he fumbled with the annoying knot that kept material between his pleasure-giving hands and the rosy nipples which were hardening, demanding to be touched. She was, in fact, too deliriously busy herself, exhilarating in the feel of the crisp, dark hair that fringed his collar, stroking the tensed muscles that rippled and heated beneath his shirt as her hands and fingers feathered and caressed them. His breathing, she noted with vague, sensuous pleasure, was as ragged as hers; their hearts seemed to pound together in a furious, deafening roar, and even the pines that cushioned them seemed to disappear. All that she was aware of was him — the weight of his hard, lean form pressing into her soft one, molding her to him, demanding and giving. The knot finally gave; his hot kisses came to her breasts as they fell like exotic fruits to his hands. His thumb, gentle but ever so slightly rough, taunted one ripe-hard nipple while his teeth reverently grazed the other, and a sob of sheer, exquisite physical pleasure escaped Sloan as she instinctively clutched his head to her with fevered fingers imbedded in his dark hair.

A twig suddenly snapped, as loud as a rifle shot in the silent glen. Sloan started, but it was Wesley who pulled away, his expression tenderly sheepish.

"Just a twig," he chuckled, after perusing their haven with a keen and astute eye. His smile was wide with understanding amusement as he watched Sloan redden and hastily retie her top with nervous, trembling fingers. "Just a twig," he repeated softly, drawing a gentle finger along her cheek.

Sloan met his tender gaze briefly, then her lashes fluttered and she stared at the ground, shielding her confusion from his view. He thought he understood, but he didn't. It was not the idea that they may have been discovered in their intimate embrace that wracked her mind with horror and left her heart sputtering erratically, her nerves tense with torment.

It was the embrace itself; the wild abandon in which she had so eagerly fallen into his arms, willing — no! desperately desiring — to give him all.

In the middle of a public park.

What had happened to her?

Had she been so lonely that she had simply craved the first attractive male to come her way? No, she had dated a number of men, persistent ones at that! They had always left her feeling nothing, not even pleasant sensations. Wesley had awakened desires which had long lain dormant within her; his touch had brought to life a warm, feeling, responsive woman — a woman Sloan had thought long dead.

In fact, in all honesty, he had aroused her to greater passion than she had felt in all her twenty-nine years, and they hadn't even . . .

Sloan breathed shakily. She had to get a grip on herself! Some huntress she was! But there was no denying the fact that Wesley was a supremely powerful and sensual man or that an undeniable chemistry existed between them. And, in a way, that was good. She would be able to bring him something honest in their marriage. Her blush, which had begun to recede, came back full force.

She wanted him with every bit as much fervor as he wanted her. She could openly give him passion.

But as he laughingly helped her to her feet and brushed away the pine needles and grass that stuck to her hair and clothing, she guiltily realized that all she could offer would not really be enough.

Wesley was a good man, an exceptionally good man — kind, gentle, understanding, and unassuming. He had survived celebrity status and wealth and retained compassion and kept a solid, worldly-but-uninflated head upon his shoulders.

He deserved everything that a wife should give; friendship, partnership, passion and — love.

Yet even as remorse filled her heart, he was tilting her head with firm persuasion, forcing her tremulous blue eyes to meet his sea-jade stare.

"Please don't look like a maiden in shock," he entreated earnestly, the dimple flashing in his cheeks. He was still amused, but her silence was causing him considerable concern.

Sloan opened her mouth to speak, but the ache in her heart caused the words to freeze on her lips. He shook his head, his smile stretching across his taut, bronzed features. She wondered fleetingly why he had to look so darned attractive just then, so masculine and virile, yet boyish with his dark hair disarrayed, his eyes dazzling mischievously, his crooked smile engagingly intent. He was twisting her apart.

But again, he was — luckily for her! — misinterpreting her reactions.

"I love you, Sloan," he said huskily. "I told you before, my intentions are entirely honorable. Years ago, I fell in love with a wisp of a girl, an infatuation, if you will. But the dream of that girl has stayed with me all my life, paling all others. And she had her own dream, and it had to be followed.

"But now, I've found her again. We're

both older and wiser. And now I know I can help her with whatever her future dreams might be. I have no intention of letting her get away again!" He kissed her again, very lightly, very tenderly, very gently. "You may think I'm crazy, Sloan, and maybe I am. I may be totally insane where you are concerned. But I do love you. I want to marry you. I know it's too early to expect an answer from such a crazy proposal, but after what just happened, I thought I should let you know how very much you do mean to me."

Sloan managed a sick, weak smile. She had won, just like that. She had taken the victory before the battle, accomplished everything she had set out to achieve — in less than three days.

Then why, she wondered miserably, was that victory so bitter-tasting, her triumph so hollow?

Had he really been in love with her for years? Was that why he had never married? Or was it talk, the bantering type of talk that lovers often used?

She really didn't know which would make her feel worse, but now, for certain, she couldn't let Wesley go.

But nor could she rid herself of a nagging feeling of . . . of . . .

Was it fear?

# CHAPTER FOUR

Sloan slid a towel around her neck and closed the door to Fine Arts 202 behind her. She shook her head slightly. Melanie Anderson and Harold Persoff were in that studio practicing to Steely Dan, while the strains of Bach were also filtering through to her from Fine Arts 204 where Gail Henning — a student determined to be the next American prima ballerina — was also at work rehearsing.

Sloan's lips curved into a slight smile. She didn't mind teaching; in fact she loved it. Gail Henning was going to make a fine ballerina, and Sloan was playing a part in making the girl's dream a reality. It was a nice feeling.

Her smile slipped and she sighed. The problem with teaching was the college. The Fine Arts department was on a low budget — in the present economy state-funded schools couldn't afford much for the arts. Theater, dance, and music — and even visual arts — were just not practical courses of study in the world the kids would face when they left. Sloan agreed with the theory that her students — even the best — should have a sound education to fall back on. She, more than anyone, knew that they would have a struggle surviving in their chosen field. But although Jim Baskins was a great department head, he was under the chairman of Fine Arts, who was under the dean, who was under the vice-president of the school, and so forth. The politics in her job drove her crazy.

She mused over the budget wars recently fought in the last faculty meetings as she entered the ring of offices shared by theater and dance, thanking the student secretary for her messages and following the labyrinth of cubbyholes until she found her own — an eight-by-eight square with a small desk and two chairs. The rest of the proposals for dance finals awaited her approval, and she slipped into a sweat shirt, chilled now by the air conditioning in her damp leotard and tights, before seating herself to concentrate on the projects. A chosen few would be previewed on Saturday when she and Jim made their own contributions to the welfare of the Fine Arts department at the annual performance. And time, Sloan thought with a grimace, was slipping away. Wrinkling her nose with distaste at the loss of time she so often endured with the red tape of the paperwork, Sloan focused her attention on what actually constituted teaching.

Sloan picked up the first folder and pursed her lips in a tolerant grimace as she saw that Susie Harris wanted to tap her final to the Doobie Brothers' "A Fool Believes." The music wasn't conducive to tap, but Sloan believed in letting the kids — kids! they were eighteen to twenty, young adults — try their wings and learn from their own mistakes. Besides, she had seen some very good work come out of the highly improbable.

Sloan scribbled a few lines of advice on Susie's folder and set it aside. Dan Taylor wanted to do a modern ballet to Schubert. . . .

Sloan set the folder down. Her effort to concentrate was fading. Chewing the nub of her pencil, she thought back to the previous night and Wesley. He hadn't mentioned marriage again; he hadn't touched her again. He had returned their relationship to a casual one, idly discussing the upcoming school performance. At her home he had played with the kids, picked up Florence, and left, saying nothing about seeing her again. . . .

The tip of the eraser broke off in her mouth, and Sloan wrinkled her face in distaste before ruefully plucking the rubber from her tongue. She was going to have to stop being such a nervous wreck — and definitely improve her hunting technique. Wesley was supposed to think of nothing but her all day long, not vice versa. And she had been thinking of nothing but Wesley all day, to the extent that her students must be thinking Mrs. Tallett was mellowing. She was considered the roughest taskmaster in the department, knowing that only grueling work could take even the most talented to the top.

In all dance classes, you perspired.

In Mrs. Tallett's classes, you *sweat!*

Sloan was aware that her budding Nureyevs thought her a strict drill sergeant, but she was totally unaware that they were devoted to her and many considered her a miracle in a small college. Half the males in her classes were also in more than a little bit of puppy love with her. She was beautiful, tall, svelte, sophisticated, and although her voice could be a cutting whip, it was a soft-spoken voice. She was tireless and demanding, but she had the grace of movement they all strove for, and she participated in her own strenuous workouts.

If you got out of Mrs. Tallett's classes alive, you had a good chance of making it as a dancer.

Today, she had been mellow. She had been busy throwing her energies into furious movement, hoping she could exhaust her frame from remembering the burning touch that had made her forget everything else.

A soft tap on her door became persistent and sharp before she heard it. "Come in," she called quickly.

It was Donna, the student-assistant secretary, and her pretty round face seemed somewhat in awe.

"What is it, Donna?" Sloan asked.

"He's here, Mrs. Tallett. To see you," Donna said disbelievingly.

Sloan frowned, sighed, and forced herself to be patient. "He *who* is here to see me, Donna?"

"Adams. The quarterback. Wesley Adams, the quarterback!" Donna said the name with awe, then rambled on, "Oh, Mrs. Tallett! He's gorgeous! What a hunk! And so nice. And he's here! Right here in Gettysburg. To see you. Oh, Mrs. Tallett, what do you suppose he wants?"

Sloan couldn't prevent the rueful grin that spread across her features. She lowered her eyes quickly, not to allow Donna to view the self-humor she was feeling. She might be the attractive and judicial Mrs. Tallett, but she was still a teacher, a mature if sophisticated woman.

Wesley was a national hero, living in the never-never land of eternal youth. It was hard to accept the fact that her students would think of her as a Cinderella chosen by the godlike prince in a miraculous whim of luck, but that was how they would see it.

"Donna," Sloan said with tolerant patience, "Wesley Adams is from Gettysburg — and he no longer plays football. And yes, he is a very nice man. Show him back, will you please?"

"Sure thing!" Donna's huge, cornflower-blue eyes still held wonder, and she hesitated as she backed out of the room.

"What else, Donna?" Sloan asked with a raised brow.

"Could you . . . would you . . . I mean, I'd love . . ."

"Love what?" Sloan prompted, holding in her exasperation.

"An autograph," Donna breathed quickly.

"I'm sure he'll be happy to give you an autograph." Sloan smiled. "He can stop back by your desk on the way out and write what-

94

ever you wish. Okay?"

"O — kay!" Donna grinned and disappeared.

Only as the door closed did Sloan realize she was once again a mess. Her leotard, tights, and leg warmers were at least new and unfaded, but her hair was drawn back in a severe bun, and the sweat shirt she wore was an old and tattered gray one. Her makeup had been through Monday's schedule — Ballet III, Jazz II, Modern I, Advanced Tap, and Aerobics. So had her body.

And it would take Donna about fifteen seconds to walk back to the central office, another fifteen or twenty to return. . . .

Sloan made a dive beneath her desk for her handbag and hastily gave herself a light mist of Je Reviens and glossed her lips quickly with a peach-bronze shade that matched her nails. Tendrils of hair were escaping the knot at her nape, but it was too late to worry. She had been thinking of Wes all day, but never expecting to see him.

The raps came on her door again, and she shoved her purse back beneath the desk. "Come in."

A giggling and blushing Donna pushed open the door and led Wesley in. Sloan could immediately see why the girl had been so taken. Wes had dressed for business today, and he was stunningly, ruggedly good-looking in a way which could let no one wonder which was the stronger, virile sex. In a navy three-piece suit, stark white shirt, and burgundy silk tie, he looked every inch the cool, shrewd businessman while still exuding an aura of an earthy power. Very civil — his omniscient-seeming green eyes were light, his grin warm — while still conveying that raw, almost primitive masculinity that women, no matter how liberated, sought in a male.

He smoothed back the breeze-ruffled silver-tinged hair that was the only thing out of context with his sleekly tailored appearance as he entered her office, overpowering everything in the small space. "Hi. I hope I'm not disturbing you. Do dance teachers get off at five like the rest of the work force?"

Sloan rose and smiled. "Not always, but you're not disturbing me." He was disturbing her, but not as he thought.

Donna still stood in the doorway, agape at their casual greetings. "Thank you, Donna." Sloan dismissed her gently. She cast a quick, apologetic glance Wes's way. "Mr. Adams will stop by your desk on the way out."

Wesley quirked a puzzled brow but agreed with her, smiling to the girl. "Sure, I'll stop by on my way out."

"Thank you," Donna murmured, flushed and pleasantly pink as she closed the door.

"Why *am* I stopping by on my way out?" he asked playfully as he took the one chair before Sloan's desk and they both seated themselves.

"An autograph. I hope you don't mind."

Dark brows knit loosely above Wes's ever-changing green eyes. "I don't mind at all, but I wasn't planning on leaving. Not without you."

"Oh?" Sloan felt her heart begin to pound harder.

"I was hoping you'd come to dinner with me."

The pounding became thunderous. She certainly couldn't pat herself on the back for playing the femme fatale too well, but he was coming to her anyway. Had he really cared something for her all those years? It was impossible to tell whether he spoke with meaning or if his words were the pleasant, teasing games that all men — she thought — played. All men except Terry. She couldn't think about Terry right now, but unfortunately, neither could she accept Wesley's invitation. She had nothing tangible to go on yet, and she had commitments she couldn't disregard even if she did.

"Wesley," she murmured unhappily, "I'd

love to go to dinner with you, but I can't. Jim and I do a dance as well as the students, and I need a little practice time by myself. And I have to pick up the children and spend time with them and feed them —"

"I've already taken all that into consideration," Wesley interrupted her, giving her his dazzling, lopsided grin. He leaned his elbows upon her desk to draw closer, and the effect of his nearness was mesmerizing. "We'll pick up the kids together and run to your house so that you can shower and change. Then we'll take the kids over to the steak house, come back so that you can spend time with them and practice, and then we'll go out. Florence will be ready anytime we are. And you won't have to worry about your time with your children — they'll be in bed before we go. We won't stay out late — I know morning comes quickly on working days."

Sloan stared into his eyes feeling a bit of awe and wonder herself. She may not be in love with Wesley, she decided, but she couldn't recall liking or even respecting a man more! He was one of the most sensitive men she had ever met, understanding in every way, not just tolerating her children, but taking great care to keep their needs at the top of his priority list.

"You are marvelous!" she whispered, and she meant every word. Another smile spread slowly across her delicately boned face, erasing the tension and strain of the day. "Thank you, Wesley," she murmured tentatively, strangely humbled by his thoughtfulness.

"For what?" he demanded, his gentle, probing green stare telling her all that she needed to know even as he brushed her gratitude aside as unnecessary.

"For understanding," she said softly.

He chuckled, but his strong features were intense, and she was left to wonder about the depths of his sincerity. "I don't have much time to convince you that I'm madly in love with you and should forever after be the only man in your life. Come on, we'll take my car and worry about yours later."

Sloan smiled a little uneasily and straightened the folders on her desk. She would deal with them in a much better frame of mind in the morning. "The entire evening sounds beautifully planned," she said huskily. "Just give me two minutes to check out with Jim and five minutes to hop into the shower."

"Take fifteen," Wes laughed, rising. "I'll go take care of your dancing football fan."

There was more than one fan in the office by the time Sloan had slipped out the back of the maze to the showers and returned to go over a few notes with Jim. Some type of student radar had gone out, and an ensemble of dancers in tights and actors in various stages of costume from the drama classes had formed in a loose circle around Wes.

As she listened to him deal politely and quietly with the students, Sloan realized that the pleasant, low-timbered quality of his voice was truly becoming dear to her. Wes Adams did have everything; sinewed good looks, personality, charisma.

And a fortune.

She must have been blind all those years ago, but then they had been young. Neither had been what they were today.

Nervousness rippled through Sloan as she silently watched him. Cassie had probably been right — Wes could crook a little finger and have any woman he wanted. For some obscure reason he wanted her, and God help her, she wanted him too, even if the feeling wasn't love. But he had to love her, really love her, because it had to be marriage . . . she *needed* him. Desperately now, now that she had let the dream grow.

Her fingers clenched at her side. She was going to have to be so very careful . . . he had to keep wanting her. For a lifetime. And he had to keep believing in the illusion she hoped she was weaving.

An illusion of assurance, of sophisticated confidence. Of having every bit as much to offer in a relationship as he.

Green eyes suddenly met hers over a sea of faces. The lazy, incredibly sexy grin curled its way back into the strong line of his jaw. "Excuse me," he murmured to the students, and then he was at her side, leading her out as young men and women watched and echoed good-byes to them both.

For a moment Sloan was tempted to laugh. Wesley would probably never realize how he had just elevated her in the eyes of the student body.

"Nice kids," Wes said as he steered her to his Lincoln in the parking lot. "They filled me in quite a bit on you."

"Really?" Sloan raised a curious and surprised brow.

"Ummm." He grinned with amusement. "They say you're the sexiest tyrant ever to head a dance class. I assured them they were probably quite right."

"Oh," Sloan laughed, wincing as she felt a blush creep over her cheeks. "About being a tyrant — or, uh . . ." Damn! What was she saying?

"Sexy?" Wes supplied, chuckling as he

shut her door. He walked around and slid into the driver's seat. "Both," he said, smiling at her. "I know you're sexy as hell, and I can bet you can be a tyrant."

"Worried?" she queried in as light and teasing a manner as she could.

"Not at all. I can fight fire with fire, my dear."

Sloan smiled, the right reaction since his answer had been teasing in kind. Yet a little trickle of unease worked its way up her neck. Had there been a hint of steel beneath his velvet tone, or was that only an illusion of her overactive imagination? She remembered the first night at her house . . . how bluntly he had called her rude. He hadn't really been angry; he had been in complete control. Yet she shuddered at the vision of a man who possessed his dynamic force and depths of passion losing his temper.

"Where are we going?" he asked.

"Pardon?"

"Your children," he replied, patient and amused by her wandering.

"Oh . . ." Sloan gave him directions to the day-care center.

Three hours later — having fulfilled all obligation to family and art — they were back on the highway driving to a hotel outside the city limits that offered rooftop dining and dancing. It was odd, Sloan thought, casting Wes a covert glance as he drove, that she had really only known him four days. She had known him years ago, of course, but that was a vague memory. On Friday night she had thought his appearance nothing more than a nuisance. The intensity of their relationship since was strangely comforting — while also disturbing. She was nervous — one couldn't be planning on marrying a man who had no idea he was being baited without being nervous — but she was now beginning to relax. For whatever heaven-sent reason, Wesley seemed to be sincere. His patience with her situation was astounding. He also seemed to be determined to pander to her every whim with tolerant amusement. Little by little, it became apparent that her inexpert vamping was working — she could almost hope she was winding him around her little finger.

It was over rainbow trout, tenderly seasoned and cooked and perfectly garnished, that Wesley began to quiz her about Terry again.

"When you talk about your husband there's a little light in your eyes," he told her, his eyes darting to hers from the fish. "It sounds like you had the perfect marriage.

Didn't you ever argue?"

Sloan smiled, still curious that it was so easy to talk him. She sensed that the questions were relevant to their own relationship, although she wasn't sure why. She answered him honestly — there was seldom a reason to hedge because he never brought up finances.

"It was a near perfect marriage, I suppose, but we did argue." She laughed. "Terry spent lots of nights on the couch."

"On the couch?" Wes seemed surprised.

Sloan frowned slightly, perplexed at his reaction, but still smiling. "Sure. He always knew when I was really angry because I'd throw his pillow and a blanket at him. By the morning — or the morning after, at least — we were ready to converse like human beings. I thought it worked well."

"You would," Wes said, and although he kept the teasing tone in his voice, Sloan noted an edge of sternness. "You weren't the one sleeping on the couch."

"I meant we both had time to cool down," Sloan said. "You disagree with such a tactic?"

"I don't believe you can run away from the issue," Wes said, signaling their waiter for coffee. "But tell me, why do you think the marriage worked so well? Take it as research, if you like," he added with a grin. "I've only heard of or seen three really good marriages — yours, your sister's, and my brother's."

Sloan mulled the question over carefully. This talk about marriage was very tricky. Perhaps she should have told him she and Terry never argued. . . . "I don't really know. I think with Terry and me it was a question of both being artists. We loved each other, and also respected each other's need to love what we did. We both knew we wanted a family. Cassie and I lost our parents when we were just out of our teens — and I learned then, and again when Terry died, just how important sisters can be. I wanted my children to have each other. So did Terry. He was an only child, and his parents died when he was young too. We had a lot in common. And I don't think I ever saw Terry really mad. He simply didn't have a temper — which was good, because mine was terrible when I was younger!" Sloan chuckled a little sheepishly. She hadn't meant to say quite so much, and Wes was watching her now intently, the green eyes seeming to pierce through to her soul. She didn't want him seeing her soul. . . .

"You seem to have pulled yourself together," he said simply. He lit a cigarette and sat back exhaling smoke, his eyes never leaving her. "Sometimes, when people lose a loved one, they blind themselves. They forget that the person was human and turn them into a god. You remember all the good, which is wonderful, but you seem to also realize he was a man."

Do I? Sloan wondered. She wasn't sure. There was still that terrible ache in her sometimes, but oddly, since she had started seeing Wesley, it was fading. It wasn't love, not as she had known it, but she respected him, admired him, and felt a wild excitement in his arms when he touched her . . . when she heard his voice . . . when she watched his powerful, lithe movements . . .

Wes abruptly changed the subject. "Would you like to dance? Or is that a poor question after you've taught all day?"

"No." Sloan smiled. "I'd love to dance. The effect is an entirely different one on a dance floor."

It was entirely different. She loved being in this man's arms, inhaling his pleasant scent, feeling the rough material of his jacket and the hard muscles beneath her fingers. Curiously, he was a wonderful dancer, light and agile on his feet, especially for a man of his size.

Tilting her chin to his face, Sloan smiled

with a lazy happiness. "You do quite well on a dance floor, Mr. Adams."

"Thank you," he replied with a shade of amusement, his hand tightening upon the small of her back and pulling her closer. "I like to think it's because of the ballet classes I've taken."

"Ballet? You?" Sloan queried with disbelief.

"Yep." They made a dip, and Sloan found her form fitting to his with uncanny perfection. "My coach made the whole team take dance classes to improve our coordination." He shrugged ruefully. "I'm six four and two hundred and twenty pounds — small compared to half the team. Seriously, imagine a guy we called Bull Bradford. Six foot eight, three hundred pounds. If a guy like that fell on one of his own teammates, he could put a player out for the entire season."

Sloan laughed and her eyes met his again. It was so good to be with him, laugh with him, have him take the burdens of her life off her shoulders. Good to be held by him, even if she held herself in careful restraint. The heat of him aroused so much in her, and she wondered fleetingly if it was wrong to want a man so badly whom she didn't love. It didn't matter, because she couldn't have him, not until . . . until he married her. She just couldn't take risks. She had always been confident in her sexuality before, but she had loved Terry, and he had loved her. What if . . . what if she just didn't have the experience or expertise to hold a man like Wesley? She shivered suddenly. She would be confident of Wesley's love when she had his ring around her finger . . . when her ragged existence had been eased.

And somehow, somehow, she thought guiltily, she would repay him. . . .

He took her to dinner again the next night, telling her in his light, easy fashion that he was staging a whirlwind courtship. He had not taken her into his arms again with the same passion he had hungrily displayed in the park; he was restraining himself. He kissed her good-night with gentle, sensual persuasions leaving her senses reeling, her body aching for the demand she had known so briefly.

Apparently, she thought ruefully as she tossed in bed after that night, her body was unaware that a winner-take-all game was being played. Thank heaven Wesley was treading lightly. She feared an edge of pressure could bring capitulation from traitorous flesh.

Summer was a big time for tourists in Gettysburg, and on Wednesday morning

Sloan noticed the traffic becoming heavy, the streets thronging with visitors. Fairly certain that Wesley would appear after her last class and ask her out for the evening, she decided to take things into her own hands. With that resolution for initiative, she planned a barbecue at her home. Wesley sounded pleasantly agreeable when she called him at the business number he had given her — they could avoid any crowds.

Jim popped his head into her half-open office doorway just as she was finishing her call. "A barbecue, eh? Am I invited?" he teased.

"Do you know," Sloan mused, wondering if it would now be a good idea to chance being alone with Wes once the little Talletts were tucked into bed, "you just gave me an idea. Yes, you are invited. Most definitely."

"Sloan," Jim demurred, sliding into her extra chair and unabashedly casting his legs — covered by woolen leg warmers — over the corner of her desk, "I was teasing. The student grapevine tells me — since you haven't bothered to" — he interrupted himself with the woeful aggrievance — "that Mrs. Tallett is running hot and heavy with Wesley Adams. Granted, I told you I was living to see this day; but seriously, shouldn't you be alone?"

"No," Sloan said firmly. "And I'm not running 'hot and heavy' with anyone." Her lips quirked into a dry smile. "I'm assuming that was a student expression?"

Jim shrugged. "Sometimes the students have apt expressions. I know you were out with him Sunday, Monday, and Tuesday. I think that qualifies for hot and heavy. Especially with you."

"Damn," Sloan murmured, "that's some grapevine. How did you know about Sunday?"

"Jeannie Holiday — my Monday Beginning Jazz class," Jim told her with a smile. "She saw you at the park."

Sloan flushed a little and made a show of straightening her desk, wondering exactly how much Jeannie Holiday had seen. "And Fine Arts majors are notoriously creative," she said lightly. "Are you going to come?"

Jim hunched his shoulders. "Wouldn't miss it," he said with a broad grin. "Sloan Tallett finally gets her rich man."

"What?" Sloan's eyes flew to his guiltily.

"The man's as rich as Onassis," Jim said. "Surely you knew that."

"I knew he was . . . comfortable," Sloan said, finding it hard to hide her conscience before Jim. She returned her attention to her desk until she could compose her features into a mask of cheerfulness. "I'm going to have Cassie and George over too . . . and my nephews, of course. Since you're coming, Jim" — she gave him a conniving smile — "do you think you could just assign my last class to their rehearsals? I'd like to hop out a little early and plan."

"Sure," Jim said agreeably. "Leave when you're ready. I'm so anxious to see this, I'll even bring the wine."

Sloan graced him with a tongue-in-cheek smile. "Bring beer — Wesley's bringing wine."

"Will do, kiddo." Jim stood and shook his head in disbelief. "I didn't think even a millionaire could get you away from those memories of yours this fast."

Sloan watched him leave her office with surprise. It was true, and Jim had seen it. She hadn't lost her memories in the last few days, but she had shelved them away in a poignant past where they belonged.

Her last-minute midweek barbecue turned out to be a wonderful success. She had overextended herself a little on the preparations, but then she decided, as the saying goes, it takes money to make money.

And she wanted Wes to think her capable of hostessing a nice, if informal, affair.

The July sun stayed out a long time, enabling the party to eat on the lawn. Sloan was thankful for her sister's appearance; with Cassie and George coming early with their two boys, she had left the supervision of all the children to them and managed to do a nice job of sprucing up the house and herself. By the time Wes had arrived, she had been cool and collected, her mad dash to collect children, clean house, and primp a thing of the past. She met him at the door with a brilliant smile, casually dressed in jeans and a body-hugging T-shirt that lent her an aura of feminine nonchalance.

When the food had been consumed and the grown-ups — including an eagle-eyed Jim — were leisurely relaxing in various stages of comfort on the back patio, George, an avid armchair quarterback all his life, talked Wesley into a football game.

"I need a handicap, though," George admitted cheerfully. "I get Jim, and I guess I have to take Cassie" — he paused with a grimace as Cassie frowned and whacked his shoulder — "and you get Sloan."

Wes chuckled and angled his head toward Sloan. "What do you say?"

Sloan shrugged with a slow smile. "Sure. If you can play ballerina, I guess I can be a halfback!"

"Go easy, halfback," Jim warned, and Sloan was startled into seeing her friend's appraising eyes on her. "Don't forget we have a performance on Saturday. I'm not dancing with a partner on crutches."

Sloan smiled at him, but her smile was uneasy. She felt he was warning her about more than a game.

"Touch game, only," Wes said, a semismile, warmly insinuative, on his lips as he cast a protective arm around Sloan's shoulders.

"And watch who you're touching where!" Cassie interjected, giving her husband an elbow in the ribs. She looked at the group with feigned grievance. "I think the man would love to get his hands on my sister!"

"Cassie!" George and Sloan gasped the protest together.

"I'm kidding, I'm kidding!" Cassie moaned. She laughed, half in earnest, half in jest. "I don't think he'd dare turn the wrong way at the moment, anyway! Wesley could fell him with one twitch of the finger."

"Hey!" George grumbled as they ambled away to form their team. "I'm not in that bad a shape — am I?"

Neither Wesley nor Sloan got to hear his wife's reply. They were laughing and forming their own huddle.

Wesley spelled out their plans for action to a giggling Sloan, who didn't understand a single play. "Woman," Wes groaned, "I'm glad you were never on the team. However" — his arms tightened excitingly around her and his whisper, warm and moist against her ear, inflamed her body from head to toe — "I never enjoyed a huddle like I'm enjoying this one."

The mini football game was fun. She and Wes had the advantage of his speed and prowess, and George had the advantage of a third person. Even with her frequent fumbles, though, she and Wes won the game. Or rather, Wes won the game. She was almost useless, but all of Wes's grumbling was good-natured. Eventually, as the summer sun faded entirely, they all wound up back where they had started — lazily sprawled around the patio, hot and pleasantly tired and thirstily finishing up the beer.

The talk was casual. Sloan, drowsy from an entire day of physical activity and rushing, didn't say much, but listened to the chatter with a feeling of well-being. She was vaguely pleased that Jim and Wes had hit it off so well. Even if she were to leave her teaching job at the college — which she intended to do if her scheming worked — he was a dear friend, one she would like to keep. Perhaps — and she allowed her mind to wander off to dreams — the two of them could form their own school one day without the miles of red tape. . . .

"Sloan?"

"Ummm!" She was nudged from dreamland by Wesley prodding the shoulder that rested against his knee.

"I'm sorry." He chuckled with affection. "I hate to disturb you with that sweet smile on your face, but I need to use the phone."

"Oh!" She jumped up quickly and excused them both from the group to lead Wes through the living room, where Cassie's boys were curled asleep on the couches, to her room and the extension. "I'll leave you to your privacy," she said, starting to close the door.

"No, stay," he said huskily, his intense green gaze demanding and sensual. "This will only take a minute, and I want to talk to you."

Sloan's heart began to flutter with anticipation and the combination of wild excitement and fear that always seemed to assail her when she was alone with him. She forced herself to smile and shrug casually before sitting idly at the foot of the bed to await his call.

It was half social call and half business,

she realized quickly. It was his brother he talked to, and he started off in a warm humor. He rattled off a few names which she assumed belonged to horses, and discussed prices and breeding stock.

Then he was silent for quite a while, listening. Sloan literally saw all warmth leave his eyes — they became hardened crystals of smooth green glass. The muscles in his face tensed and tightened; a vein began to pound furiously in the whipcord strength of his neck. His jawline was hard and squared, the total quality of his handsome features suddenly transformed into something more chilling than she had ever seen before.

A face more fierce and ruthless than she had ever imagined. Wesley Adams furious.

Despite his metamorphosis, he remained silent, his hand tightening around the receiver until his knuckles went white.

But not as white as Sloan was feeling. It wasn't directed at her, but his anger was the type that froze a person's blood. Just watching the apparent control he wielded, allowing only muscles to tighten, started a shivering inside of her that would not cease.

He spoke low — a deathly growl. "Fire him. And make sure he's off the place before I get back."

Apparently the person on the other end of

the wire knew there was no mercy when that restrained, bloodcurdling hiss was used. Wesley listened again, but Dave Adams had little else to say.

The tension in Wes ebbed somewhat as he said good-bye, his anger not directed at his brother, but at the party being fired. Sloan would hate to be that person, but if she was the employee in question, she would definitely be long gone before Wes got back.

The receiver clicked precisely back into its holder, and Sloan found herself wishing he had not asked her to stay in the room. She didn't think she wanted to hear anything he had to say at that moment, not with that look of ruthless authority still on his face.

Wes turned to her suddenly, as if just realizing she was still with him. "I'm sorry," he said quietly. "We had a problem with a trainer."

For some ridiculous reason — perhaps her own shivering apprehension — Sloan felt pity for the unknown man and came to his defense, stuttering, "Wh— what happened? Perhaps you should give the man a second chance —"

Wesley interrupted her, his lips drawn in a tight white smile. "I don't give second chances. I gave him a chance when I hired him. He came in drunk, decided to take one of our most promising three-year-olds out, and caused the mare to break her leg. She had to be destroyed."

"Oh," Sloan murmured weakly. Besides the anger, she could sense the pain in his voice.

But Wes could make incredible changes. His smile and eyes became lighter as he walked to her and placed his hands on her shoulders, then tilted her chin toward his. "There's nothing more to be done about it," he said gently. "I'm sorry, I seem to have put a damper on your evening."

"No —" Sloan protested, but she didn't get a chance to say more. She was drawn up, inexorably, into his arms. There was a force to him tonight, a leftover of the coiled tension he had constrained, a shuddering that rippled through sinewed muscles and lent heat and passion to his rough but tender command. His lips taking hers with no question or persuasion but with need and mastery. His tongue invaded the moist intimacy of her mouth, expecting submission with absolute authority and receiving it.

Sloan was at first startled, and then mesmerized. She couldn't have denied him . . . had she wanted to . . . been able to . . .

His hands were as sure as his lips. With

118

one he held the small of her back, curving her to him in an arch that made her even more aware of his burning heat and his need for her, a need she felt that she melted to like soft wax. The excitement and spark of fire she experienced near him suddenly burst into flame like an inferno. His other hand was firmly caressing her face, sliding down the silken column of her neck, fondling her collarbone, her shoulder, seducing with each firm movement. It crept between them with no thought of obstruction from her to crush against her breast, seeking as it enticed, a work-roughened thumb grazing a nipple with expert enticement until it hardened to a full peak, straining against the fabric of her shirt to receive the intoxicating touch. A moan sounded in Sloan's throat, a whimper of desire. She was lost in his onslaught, swept away in a great wash of desire that began as a burning need in the root of femininity and spread a weakness rushing through her like a tidal wave. She couldn't think, only need and crave . . . from somewhere a voice inside her reminded her that she couldn't give, but it made no sense . . . she wanted desperately to give . . . and give . . . and keep on giving until she could quench the terrible storm of desire. . . .

Her fingers, limp at first, found life. They

curled over his broad shoulders, marveling at the play of muscle, and moved on to the coarse edges of dark hair at his nape, pulling her ever closer as her mind whirled in sensation. She wasn't sure that she still touched earth. . . .

She never did think of her conniving that night. It was a sudden splurge of fear, spurred as his fingers slipped beneath her shirt to sear her flesh with new pleasure that finally jolted her mind. *What if she wasn't all that he wanted? What if she froze and just couldn't . . . ?* It had been so very long. . . .

All the terrors that flitted through her mind were unnecessary. Wesley had remembered where they were and under what circumstances, even if she hadn't. He drew away with a shake, then pulled her close to his chest again with tenderness. Her head rested against his thundering heart as he spoke.

"There's so much I want to say to you, Sloan. But I think your other guests are going to start speculating as to what we're up to. I can't wait long, though. Saturday night, when your performance and the hectic pace that goes with it is over, we're going to leave George and Cassie early and find some place to be entirely alone. No crowded dance floor or restaurant, and no car. I want you alone. Agreed?"

Sloan nodded vigorously against his chest, not trusting herself to speak. Please God, she prayed hastily, let it be a proposal. I don't think I can handle this much longer. And if I'm his wife, I know I'll be okay, I'll have to be okay, because I'll know he wants me forever. . . .

Everyone left shortly after they returned to the patio, Wesley brushing a quick kiss against her forehead as he helped George carry out his sleeping sons.

Sloan slept soundly. She had weighed all Wesley's words and actions and convinced herself that he was sincere. Saturday night was sure to bring the proposal she so desperately needed.

And she had completely forgotten the other insight she had momentarily seen of the man when his temper had flared.

A man who gave no second chances and slashed offenders with a swift but merciless blow.

# CHAPTER FIVE

For some inexplicable reason the traffic in town went mad on Thursday morning. Running late to begin with, Sloan found driving the short distance to work a tedious chore. Gritting her teeth but resigned, she wove her way through vehicles that appeared ridiculously confused.

Reaching the parking lot of the college, Sloan quickly collected her things and raced into the Fine Arts building. She and Jim had a rehearsal scheduled before their first classes, and they needed every second of time. The performance was only two days away. Depositing her street clothing and papers in her office, she moved straight into Fine Arts 202, where Jim was already engaging in warm-up exercises.

"Good morning," she called quickly, making her way to the bar where she began her own series of stretches starting with limbering pliés.

"Good morning, Mrs. Tallett," Jim returned her call, his voice laced with a teasing amusement. "Or is it soon to be Mrs. Adams?"

Sloan stretched high in a relevé, watching the graceful movement of her hand from side to over her head. "Do I detect a caustic note in that query?" she asked lightly.

"Caustic? Who me? Never," Jim replied, leaping away from the bar to approach the tape player, where he set the music for their number — a medley of classical, jazz, blues, and rock created especially for them by the music department. "Ready?" he asked.

"Ready."

The music began. Sloan whirled into his arms, then spun beneath his guidance in a slow pirouette with a high kick.

"Be careful, Sloan."

Sloan missed a beat of the music and almost fell instead of swirling back into his arms. She kept her expression implacable and swirled across the floor, not answering until she returned to his side to be lifted high in the air. "I don't know what you're talking about."

"I think you do."

"I don't."

"You've got a tiger by the tail, Mrs. Tallett."

Sloan stopped the dance and walked purposefully to the tape player to halt the flow of the music, crossing her arms and facing Jim. "Okay, Mr. Baskins, let's have it. What are you talking about?"

"Oh, Sloan, don't go getting indignant," Jim said with a sigh. "I'm your friend. I'm just warning you to be careful."

"With Wesley?" It was really more of a statement than a question.

"Yes, with Wesley Adams. I watched you last night, Sloan, and I know you. I saw all those seductive smiles and that lazy sensuous charm. You're snaring your beast all right; I just hope you know what you're doing."

She could have cut Jim off by simply telling him it was none of his business, but Sloan didn't want to. He was a friend, but more than that, she had to see what he was reading from her behavior, because if she couldn't convince Jim, she feared she would never get by the astute, probing eye of Wes. . . .

"I thought you liked him," she said innocently.

"I do," Jim told her. "He's the type of man you respect immediately, and he's natural — honest. But don't fool yourself," Jim advised. "He's nothing like your Terry."

"You didn't know Terry," Sloan observed dryly.

"But I know of him — just like I know of Wes Adams," Jim said with a sigh. "I just want you to be aware that you're not dealing with the same type of man."

Sloan frowned. "I don't understand what you're getting at, Jim. Are you trying to say Wes isn't the nice person he appears to be?"

"I'm not saying that at all. From what I've read, he's even a bit of a philanthropist. But" — the warning was clear — "he's not the type of man you cross, or play with loosely."

Sloan smiled slowly but surely. Jim wasn't doubting her emotion — he was just wondering how far she planned to carry it. Scampering back across the floor to him, she planted a quick kiss on his cheek. "You can stop worrying — *Dad*," she teased. "I'm not playing loosely with him at all. And I haven't a thought in the world about crossing him."

Jim flushed. "Okay — lecture over. And please! Put the music back on! We have about fifteen minutes left."

But it was Jim who kept talking as they rehearsed. It seemed he was as well-read on Wesley Adams as Cassie. Wes, according to Jim, was a veritable tiger when it came to business. He was considered one of the most ethical men in the field of Thorough-breds, but demanding in return. He dealt fairly, and expected the same in return. Woe to the man who attempted anything less.

Sloan paid little attention to his dissertation. She was wondering if she had judged Wes to be similar to Terry. Not really, she decided. Terry and she had been little more than children at first, growing together, but still squabbling like children together. Both men were courteous, but Terry *had* been completely carefree, without a serious bone in his body, without that piercing vitality that was part of Wes.

She was startled to realize that in her comparisons, Wesley was coming out by far the stronger man. Silly, she told herself. Terry had died at twenty-eight . . . he had never had a chance to really be a man . . . not in that assured, virile sense that Wes was.

It was strange, she noted vaguely late that night as she sat with Wes on her sofa sipping coffee, that Jim had asked her if she was comparing Wes to Terry. Because Wes brought up the same subject, suddenly, abruptly.

He set his mug on the coffee table and took both her hands in his. "You know, Sloan, that I'm not Terry."

At first confused and disoriented, Sloan made a quick comeback. "Of course you're not."

He shook his head with a tender smile. "I'm mean, I don't think — in fact, I'm *sure* that I'm nothing like Terry. I want you to understand that."

Still confused, Sloan smiled, quivering inwardly at both the electricity that shot through her with the sear of his gaze and the implications of the deep sincerity of his words.

"I know you're not Terry, or not like him," she said softly. The right answer was important now she knew; every man — or woman, for that matter — wanted to be loved for what he or she was. "Terry was part of another lifetime. I loved him, but I'd never look to replace him." A slight beading of perspiration broke out across her forehead, and her hands went clammy. She needed to say more. . . . "I love you, Wes." There. It hadn't been hard, it had been incredibly easy.

And it was out . . . it was said. He intended to have her, he had told her, so she waited with anxious anticipation for his response. Surely he would take her into a passionate embrace . . . or make a new declaration in return.

Wes responded neither way, yet the intensity of his voice and the tender reverence with which he lightly lifted her chin to meet his eyes left her trembling, her mouth dry, her senses paralyzed.

"I can't tell you what hearing that means, Sloan. I think I've waited half my life to hear those words from you, and I would have waited another eternity."

Sloan tried to smile but found that she couldn't. His eyes burned into hers, deeply green, deeply charged with electric emotion. She was unable to look away, unable to release herself even as she wondered once again if he was seeing through her, reading all the thoughts and sins that existed within her soul. No, he couldn't be, because if he could read her soul, he would not be sitting there, he would be racing out the door.

He did stand, breaking the moment's spell. "I'd better run," he said, his hand settling gently on the top of her head and lightly massaging her hair against her temple. "Tomorrow is a workday for you, and I have an eight A.M. meeting a few miles out of town." He reached to grasp her hands and pull her to her feet. "Come on, walk me to the door."

Rising and slipping into the easy shelter of his arm, Sloan allowed her worry to cease.

Her mind turned to the comfort and pleasure she found with his touch and easy camaraderie.

He paused with his hand on the doorknob and looked at her with a rueful grin. "I guess this is it until Saturday night," he murmured softly.

"Oh?" Sloan queried, somewhat surprised that he wouldn't be with her the next night — and startlingly disappointed. Had she come to depend on him so much that a night away seemed like endless time?

"I have another meeting tomorrow night," he explained. "One that might not end till midnight."

"You're welcome to stop by," Sloan murmured, hearing herself say the words without thought.

"No." He smiled broadly, his eyes very gentle, as if the thought on her part had meant very much. "Your dance is on Saturday — I'm sure it's quite a rush with the children and then the students. I don't want to be the one to keep you from a peak performance, and" — he brushed a kiss against her temple — "I also have selfish reasons for wanting you well rested. I want to keep you out till all hours on Saturday night!"

"Oh," Sloan repeated, aware that her pulse was racing madly and she was anticipating his mind-numbing good-night kiss.

But again, he did the unexpected. Instead of pulling her into the tight embrace of his arms, he brushed her forehead again with the briefest of feather-light caresses. And yet, the passion was there, barely hooded by sensuously lazy lids over the ocean-deep eyes as he pulled away. "Till Saturday night," he said huskily.

Sloan watched as his tall form disappeared down the path and into his car. She was dismayed to realize that she was hopelessly frustrated. Her anticipation had taunted her senses unbearably. It was with a raw, physical pain that she watched him leave, a fervent prayer on her lips; let it be soon . . . please, let it be soon. . . .

But could she force a wedding soon enough while still pretending to be the one to fall heedlessly under the spell of a relentless pursuer?

Sloan would have never admitted it to herself, but no matter what appearances were, no matter what Wes said or did, no matter how much confidence she felt in herself as a human being and a woman, she was running a little scared. At first Wes had been little more than an appropriate pawn, but the more she saw of him, the more she became aware that she had stepped a little out of her league without really realizing it.

She would have to be very careful never to take him for granted, make any type of assumption. Ironically, where she often felt old at twenty-nine, he, just five years older, was young — no, not young, but at a "prime" age for a male. Twenty-nine wasn't old, she reminded herself — it was being a "widow" that so often made her feel so — that and the responsibility of the children.

Nevertheless, Wes had everything to offer someone, while she had nothing.

She slept in a torment that night, altering between the conviction that he really did love her, and the fear that he would wake up and discover that she was nothing but a liability. And then again she would be plagued by guilt — because all she had to offer was love — and even that she wasn't sure she could ever give, even though she enjoyed him, respected him, admired him.

The morning went all wrong, and she was glad Wes wasn't making an appearance at her house. Trying to keep up "perfect" appearances all week, she had let many things slide. She had "cleaned" every night by stuffing things under the beds or into closets — and now, as she tried to dress the children, she discovered that she seemed to be missing the mate to every shoe she found.

And she didn't seem to have a clean sock in the house for Jamie.

But eventually everyone was ready. Sloan dropped the kids off at Cassie's — they would attend the performance with their aunt, uncle, and cousins — and hurried to the school, past the Fine Arts building today, and on to the main auditorium.

Where once again she met pandemonium. The dance was a major function for the school, and the students finally chosen to be a part of the performance were, naturally, nervous and jittery. They all needed a pat on the back as Sloan went over the program.

She had heard that time could stand still, but it dismayed her to discover today that it could flash by. She barely found the minutes to slip into her own costume, a mist of striking red and blue silks, before Jim was rushing past her to announce the students. The music department was out in full to lend support with accompaniment, and Jim waited with patience while the crowd quieted after the houselights dimmed.

She and Jim were the finale. As always for Sloan, she was immediately lost in the music. She loved to dance, she lived, came alive when she danced.

But today it was something more.

She knew that Wes watched.

Every movement was for him. Each kick was a little higher, each whirl and dip and spin a touch more sensual. For the first time in her life, her dance was a calculated one, planned to seduce one man into believing she was something special, that he couldn't live without her.

The lie came home to her as the music ended and the auditorium rang with applause. Sloan, her head bowed over her knee in a split, lost the magic that had been hers as she danced. She was just a widow with three children, scrambling for a dubious existence — not in the least special.

But Wes was for real. A football hero matured into a very special man, a man with dignity, pride, compassion, strength and humor and love. . . . And she couldn't let him fall out of love with her. He had to keep believing and loving. She would make it up to him.

"Sloan." Jim nudged her with a laugh. "You can get up now — I'd hate to see you stiffen in that position. Makes walking rough."

She gave her boss a dry grimace and accepted his hand to rise. Smiling along with him, she curtsied to the audience, and together they seemed to float off the floor. "So how did we do?" she inquired briskly, lest he inquire into her mind wandering.

"Why don't you ask Mr. Adams?" Jim suggested with an inclination of his head.

"Wes!" Sloan fought hard to keep her voice from shrieking as she saw him over Jim's shoulder. "I — I thought I wasn't going to see you until tonight!"

He was impeccable as he approached her in the busy backstage wing, his tan suit a striking complement to his dark hair and deep eyes. The bronze tone of his arresting profile was never more apparent, nor the muscle tone that lurked beneath its covering. Sloan was suddenly aware that her coiled hair was damp from exertion — as was her costume. But she didn't have much time to reflect on her own appearance; he was already at her side, already talking.

"You weren't going to see me," he murmured huskily, as if temporarily unaware that Jim — or anyone else for that matter- still hovered near. "But I couldn't leave without telling you that you were magnificent. Superb. Beautiful —"

"Thanks," Jim chimed in, drawing abrupt looks from them both. Sloan frowned with annoyance, but Wes laughed. "Sorry, Jim, you weren't beautiful, but it was a hell of a performance."

The two men shook hands, and Sloan was split between being glad of their friendship while also annoyed that Wes accepted the interruption so easily. He should be a little jealous of Jim, Sloan thought fleetingly. I was dancing with him. If Wes really loved me. . . .

He did love her. Really love her. And he trusted her. He knew she needed room for her own self-expression to be all she could be, and he had the confidence to allow it.

"I'm going," he told them both quickly, glancing at the students who awaited their instructors' words before dispersing. "Jim — be seeing you. Sloan — I'll be by at about eight. I'll get George and Cassie first." With a wave he was gone, his broad-shouldered frame drawing speculative and appreciating gazes as he retreated out of the stage wings.

"Watch it, Sloan," Jim muttered mischievously. "I can see your mind ticking. The beast is wrapped around your finger, but I think it's the tail you're wrapping, and if you're not careful, he's going to feel the pull."

"Jim —" Sloan began to protest with a frown.

"I'll bet you didn't know he was a Scorpio." Jim overrode her objection. "Scorpios are known for their sting."

Sloan smiled dryly. "Go dismiss the kids, will you, Mr. Astrology. I'm not pulling tails, and I'm not going to get stung. You tell me you like the man, but then you sound as if you think he is a beast!"

"No — you misunderstand. I do like the man — maybe because there's no hedging or backing down about him. But *I'm* not in your position!" With that enigmatic advice, Jim quirked his brows and turned to the waiting students.

Sloan showered and dressed carefully, choosing a soft knit with a flaring skirt for the evening. She was nervous, knowing that this night was it — the make it or break it for herself. Qualms of conscience assailed her while she did try to convince herself that she had him wrapped around her finger.

After tucking the kids in, she returned to her own room to make a last-minute check on her appearance. The dress molded to her curvacious form like a glove; her hair, brushed from the chignon, fell about her face in soft waves, giving her the impression of innocence. Radiant happiness gave her face a beautiful glow, and she laughed uneasily.

"Maybe I am in love with him!" she told her reflection. Love was, after all, an elusive word composed of many emotions. It was also something which, nurtured correctly, could grow to endless bounds.

The doorbell rang, and she gave her dress a final straightening before running breathlessly to answer the clanging summons. Wesley filled the doorway with his imposing frame, causing her heart to skip for a second. In a black tux and sky-blue shirt he was impeccable, handsome beyond all earthly rights in a way that was still rugged and slightly savage in spite of his formal dress.

Sloan didn't realize she had been staring until his special teasing grin spread across his face and he murmured, "I think we should come in. Florence can hardly watch the children from outside!"

Sloan blushed, lowered her eyes, and moved away from the door. Wes ushered Florence inside, then followed suit himself.

"Any instructions, young lady?" Florence asked cheerfully.

"Ah . . . no," Sloan said quickly. "The kids are asleep, and you know where everything is. Make yourself at home, and Florence . . . thank you, very much."

"Nonsense!" Florence said briskly. "You two run along and have a good time. Your sister and brother-in-law are already in the car."

Sloan could not remember a more pleasant evening in her entire life. A more congenial foursome could not have existed; wine and conversation could not have flowed more fluidly. Dancing with Wes, sitting beside him and receiving his casual, intimate touch, was the most natural thing in the world. For a time she was content thinking how lucky it was that Wesley seemed to belong with her group, then she realized, with a bit of awe, that it wasn't Wesley who had found his niche, it was she. She belonged with him. And she loved that belonging. No one had ever made her feel so very alive, so vibrantly aware. Not even Terry. No, not even Terry had held her with such competent arms, had thrilled and excited her with a simple glance or possessive touch on a shoulder.

Cassie suddenly stifled a yawn with embarrassment. "Excuse me!" she apologized.

"Company boring you, huh?" George teased.

"Oh, no!" Cassie protested. "This has been the nicest night! It's just that I'm not used to late hours."

"I think that's our cue," Wes told Sloan with mischievous eyes. "Time to take the

138

Harringtons home."

George glanced at his wife, insinuatively wiggling his brows. "I'm amazed these lovebirds have taken this long, aren't you?"

"George!" Cassie remonstrated. "Hush! You're embarrassing them!"

"We're not embarrassed," Wes said with a leisurely smile. "And you're not keeping us. We've got all night."

Sloan felt as if her heart had crashed into her stomach. All night! Did he think she was spending the night with him? Her throat went dry and her hands clammy. Had she played the seductress too well? She couldn't have him pressuring her. If he pushed, she might capitulate! And then he might decide that there really wasn't anything so special about her after all. . . .

But at the moment, she was cornered. The check was paid; they were rising to leave. And she had imbibed too freely of the wine. She shook her head. Her thoughts were fuzzy, and she needed a sharp, clear mind.

As they drove to drop off Cassie and George, she was quiet and withdrawn, mentally planning strategy with a desperate speed. She was still quiet when they were finally alone, until it occurred to her that she didn't even know where they were headed.

Moistening her lips and breathing deeply, she asked with a wobbly effort at nonchalance, "Where are we going?"

Wesley's jade gaze fell to her with a burning intensity. Although he grinned with his usual ease, his voice was hoarse and husky when he replied. "The nice romantic spot I promised. My house."

Sloan became dizzy with fear. Was he wrapped around her finger as tightly as she thought? She nervously smoothed already smooth hair. At any rate, she reasoned, the man wasn't a rapist. He wouldn't force her to do anything.

But she wasn't afraid of him using force, and she knew it. She was afraid of her own reactions. Heaven help me! she prayed fervently as he ushered her toward his darkened house. But would heaven help her after all that she had done? More likely, the powers that be would listen and laugh. . . .

Wesley switched on dim lights as they entered and calmly walked ahead of her. "Brandy?" he asked, as she stood in the doorway surveying the elegant room. Wesley's taste in decor was stunning — casual and warm, but elegant. The entrance hallway, carpeted in a creamy pile, led to a sunken living room, plush with thickly cushioned, wicker furniture. Palms and ferns

140

unobstrusively added a beguiling hospitality, as did the glass window doors which led to a screened patio, complete with a sparkling, kidney-shaped pool and a whirling hot tub.

"Come in," Wesley invited with amusement, divesting himself of jacket, tie, and cummerbund and grimacing as he undid the top three buttons of his shirt. "The attack dogs have the evening off."

Sloan flushed as she moved uneasily down to the plush, sunken area. She sat, thinking she would have to remain seriously on guard in Wesley's territory. Her mind was so benumbed that she started when he handed her a snifter of brandy.

"It's me," he said kindly. "The same old Wesley you've been seeing all week." He sat beside her, sipped at his own glass, and took her chin gently with his free hand. "The same old Wesley who loves you very much," he added softly. "The same old Wesley who wants to marry you."

For some ungodly reason, she was close to tears. Without thinking, she blurted, "Why?"

"I could tell you a million things," he said, hypnotizing her with the gleaming jade of his eyes and the tender stroke of his fingers on the soft flesh of her face. "I can say because you're bright and beautiful and more graceful and lovely than any other living creature. And it will be true. But there's only one real reason — the only reason anyone should ever marry. Because I love you. I want to share my life with you. I want to be a part of yours."

The tears finally streamed down Sloan's cheeks. "Oh, Wesley . . ."

"Hey! I didn't mean to make you cry!" he exclaimed gently, setting their brandies aside and taking her comfortingly into his arms. He rocked her soothingly and stroked the lush tendrils of hair from her forehead. "Hey!" he repeated softly. "Don't cry. Just answer me. I won't rush you, but I'll go clear out of my mind if I keep thinking that maybe you will when you don't —"

"I will!" Sloan interrupted quickly. What the hell was she doing? she demanded of herself. She was crying like an idiot, feeling like a complete louse, just because he had said a few sentimental things. And why? He wanted her, he loved her. She wouldn't be twisting his arm.

The only reason . . . he had said. Love. That was why. She was betraying him in the most cruel way possible.

Hating herself, she lifted sapphire eyes to his. "I will marry you, Wesley. There's nothing I want more."

His arms tightened around her. "When?" he gasped hoarsely.

"As soon as possible," she replied. "To-morrow, if we could. . . ."

He was startled, but pleasantly so. She knew he had expected her to set a date months in the future.

"Monday we'll get the license," he promised her. "And a week from today, we'll become man and wife." His lips fell upon hers with a passionate urgency, plundering the softness of her mouth. Sloan moaned faintly beneath his assault, in agony as she tried to keep a clear head. It was almost impossible. His crisp, clean scent was intoxicating her, his hands were arousing her to a feverish pitch as they roamed to secret places and sought her body through the field of silk.

Somehow, without her even knowing it, Wes had found the zipper to her dress and the silk fell from her with a whispered rustle. She heard his sharp intake of breath, then felt the pressure of his hands as he forced her down to the pillowy cushion of the couch. His hot kisses, hungry and out of control, blazed paths across her flesh. As if she were intoxicated, it slowly filtered into Sloan's mind that they were fast reaching a point of no return. Even as she stumbled mentally, Wesley's sure fingers found the front clasp of her lacy bra, and it joined the silk dress on the floor. His mouth found the firm flesh of her breasts, teased and raked her nipples until she cried out with an agony of despair and longing. She wanted him so desperately! To stop the excruciating pleasure would be to bring excruciating pain.

His hand ran along her leg, causing her to shake uncontrollably. Her slip wound around her waist; his hand found the elastic of her panties, and she gasped at the surge of desire awakened within her at the touch of his fingers so low on her abdomen, a touch which caused her to inadvertently strain toward him.

Then the ultimate warning in her head finally sounded. He was still clothed, but his knee was wedging firmly between hers, and his hand was subtly but surely exploring further. Bracing herself firmly, Sloan finally found her voice, begging him to stop.

At first she was totally ignored. Terror that she had played too closely with fire surged through her, and she gripped her fingers painfully into his hair. "Please, Wesley!" she sighed. "I beg you!" Tears formed again in her eyes and cascaded down her cheeks. "Please!" she whispered.

Wesley went rigid; his harsh breathing

gave her the answer that he had at last heard her plea.

He didn't speak as he lifted his weight from her and tossed her discarded clothing into her lap. He didn't even look at her until she had reclasped her bra and slipped hurriedly back into her black silk dress.

Then he sat beside her, and she knew when he probed her face with an icy green stare that he was angry. But he didn't yell, he didn't make recriminations. He sat with folded arms and demanded. "Why?"

"I — I just can't!" she croaked shamefully.

"Go on," he prompted grimly.

Her abject misery was not, at the moment, a performance. Her hands were trembling so badly she could barely get a sip of sorely needed brandy to her lips. Yet still, her mind was ticking away with all speed. Her answer would have to be good. Looking tentatively at Wesley, she shivered and her eyes fluttered closed. *Think!* she told herself. She had everything at stake in the next few minutes.

"Please, tell me what's wrong," he persisted, and she chanced another glance into his probing jade orbs. He had gentled, his voice had become the kind one she was accustomed to hearing.

Taking a few deep breaths, she decided

she could almost be honest. Looking straight into her brandy, she plunged ahead with a shy, very convincing explanation for her behavior which bordered on truth.

"I'm frightened, Wesley. I don't know what impression I give, but I've been alone for a long time." She knew she was blushing profusely. "The only man I've ever known was Terry, and — well, we were married. I know that sounds ridiculously old-fashioned, but . . ."

Wesley emitted a strangled sound, and Sloan glanced at him, cringing, fearing she had pushed his patience too far. But he was no longer angry, he was chuckling.

"What's so funny?" she queried with piqued exasperation.

"Nothing, darling, nothing," he assured her. He sat beside her again, ran his fingers through his dark hair, and took her hand to idly massage her fingers. "I don't think you're ridiculously old-fashioned. I'm kind of glad. I'd be insanely jealous if I had to learn about your other lovers. I'm even jealous of Terry, although God knows I can't begrudge the man a thing. He had heaven on earth and he had to lose it." His eyes met hers. "I laughed because you had me frightened too. I thought you might have a serious hang-up about *me*. If marriage is

146

important to you before making a sexual commitment, I can honor that. That is" — he chuckled again, the throaty sound that was deep and endearing — "as long as you are sure that you do want me when we are married and as long as we do hurry with the wedding!"

Sloan stared at him with wide, blank eyes. "I do want you, Wes, I want you more than I've ever wanted another human being."

"I'm all yours, darling," he swore, with a light kiss on her forehead. "But I'd better get you home, because I want you to be all mine. All of you," he added, running a finger along the flesh of her bare arm. "Every delightful inch!" He kissed the tip of her nose. "Just one week . . ."

Sloan continued to shiver all the way home. Just one week. Then it would be pay-up time. And she had the strange feeling that, once she had legally sold herself to Wesley Adams, there would be no backing down.

Ever again.

# CHAPTER SIX

Sloan called in late on Monday morning, and within an hour she and Wesley had filled in all the necessary papers and taken blood tests. Wes suggested they stop for a bite to eat before she went in to work as there were a few things he wanted to discuss.

"I've got to drive home for a few days," he told her as he folded his menu and handed it to the waitress. At her look of surprise he continued, "We'll be going on a honeymoon. I need to cover myself and get back to Kentucky and check with my brother on the farm. I also want to tell him about us first-hand and talk him and my sister-in-law into coming up for the wedding."

Sloan was startled. She had almost forgotten that Wes had another home and a family. "When are you leaving?" she asked unhappily. She was surprised at how it hurt to know they'd be parted. In a short time, Wes had come to pleasantly dominate her life, and she hadn't even realized it.

"Today," he replied with a cross between a smile and a leer. "I won't be back until Friday, which is probably best for both of us! I won't be trying to attack you every night, and you won't have to worry about fighting me off!"

"Oh, Wes!" Sloan murmured miserably.

"Hey! I'm teasing!" He chuckled, tenderly lifting her chin. "I have to take care of this now, though, because I don't want to worry about anything after the wedding. Where would you like to go?"

"Pardon?"

"Our honeymoon, darling," he said with a patient grin. "Is there anywhere particular you'd like to go?"

"Ah — no," Sloan stammered. She hadn't even thought about a honeymoon. In fact, she hadn't really thought about anything beyond the wedding.

"Then I have a suggestion. I have a friend who recently bought a hotel just outside of Brussels. He swears it's one of the most beautiful cities in the world, and he's surrounded by hilly forests and sparkling little streams. We can spend a week there, and then a week in Paris. How does that sound?" Wesley sipped his coffee and watched her over the rim of his cup.

"It sounds lovely," Sloan replied with a

slow smile. Belgium and France! She had never been out of the eastern United States! Wesley was opening doors for her which she had never even dreamed existed. "But, what about the children?"

"Florence will watch them, of course," Wes told her with a wave of his hand. "I'll have her move her things into your house tonight so that she can get used to your routine. Cassie and George will be around if anything she can't handle comes up, and hopefully, Dave and Susan will be here with their kids, and Jamie, Laura, and Terry can meet their new cousins and aunt and uncle. My sister lives in Arizona near my folks, so I doubt if she'll be able to make it or my mom and dad for that matter." He grimaced as he idly ran a finger over the top of her hand. "Dad has a heart condition, so he doesn't travel frequently. We'll fly out to meet them in a few months."

Sloan's head was reeling. There were so many things she hadn't taken into consideration! A small chill knotted in her stomach. "Wes," she said slowly. "What happens when we come back? Do we" — she licked dry lips — "Do we move to Kentucky?" Kentucky, away from everything she knew, away from Cassie and George. It almost sounded like an alien planet! And what about his family? What if they disliked her? What if they resented her barging into their lives with a household of children? What if they felt she were too old for Wes, too encumbered? His parents would want him to marry a younger girl, she was sure, one who would provide him with his own family.

Wesley's hand was warm over hers. As usual, he was reading the worries she couldn't voice aloud. "I promise you," he guaranteed her softly. "You'll love Kentucky. So will the kids. And my brother is a wonderful guy; Susan's terrific. We'll be in the same house for a while, but don't worry, it's huge. You don't have to see anyone else if you don't want to. I'll have George put my house here on the market while we're gone, but we'll keep yours and spend as much time in Gettysburg as we can. Okay?"

The secure pressure of his hand filled her with contentment. "Okay."

"And," he added with a conniving wink, "we have several good, professional dance companies in the nearby cities."

"Bribery will get you everywhere!" Sloan laughed happily. Wes *was* magic. He could work everything out.

Their sandwiches arrived, and Sloan found she had a good appetite for her ham and cheese. She was going to miss Wes terribly, but as he had said, his absence would be for the best. When he came back, there would be less than twenty-four hours left for anything to go wrong!

They discussed a few more details as they ate. The wedding would take place at Wesley's house with just their families and a few close friends in attendance. Sloan was to cater whatever she wanted, as long as she didn't put a strain on herself. After a quick reception, they would fly overseas right away.

"Oh! One more thing," Wesley added, his green eyes twinkling like gemstones as he reached into his vest pocket for a small jewel case. Flicking it open with one hand, he gently took her slim fingers with the other and slid the ring from the velvet box. "I'd like you to start wearing this," he said, extracting first the plain gold band which had adorned her finger since the day Terry had put it on. Then his ring went on, and Sloan stared at her finger with a mixture of nostalgia and joy. Terry's ring was gone. But Terry was gone, and somehow it didn't hurt so badly anymore. Oh, his memory would always sadden her; he had been her youth, her first great love, the father of her three children. But nothing could bring him back. She would always remember him with love, but . . . her eyes widened with shock. Water filled within them, but she was laughing too, with pure happiness. The loss of her love didn't hurt so much anymore because she had found new love without even knowing as it snuck up on her. She wanted to scream and shout with the joy of her realization, but Lord! Wes would never understand. Instead, she clutched his large hand in hers and covered it with tearstained, sloppy kisses. "Oh, Wes!" she murmured breathlessly, mindless if the other patrons of the coffee shop thought her crazy or not, "I do love you so!"

"And I love you, my dearest princess," he whispered in return, taking her hands tenderly to his mouth to kiss them reverently. Then the teasing glimmer leaped back into his eyes as he studied the ring objectively. "Perfect, if I do say so myself." It was a diamond, probably about two carats, Sloan judged, surrounded by a bed of sapphires. He traced the circle of blue stones with his fingers. "For your eyes, love. They match incredibly well." He released her hand reluctantly. "You'd better get into work so that you can quit, and I'd better head out of town. Or else, darling," he said huskily, one sensual dark brow raised in a rakish angle, "I shall carry you from this table and savagely ravish you in the back seat of the Lincoln."

Sloan half smiled with a rueful quirk of her lips and angled a furrowing brow herself. "I don't think I'd mind being ravished in the Lincoln," she murmured in teasing reply, fully aware that she now meant her words with no qualms. Love may not conquer all, but it did sweep away her doubts and insecurities. "But I've got a problem, Wes. I can't just quit my job. I'm a teacher. Jim can cover me for a couple of weeks, but I have to go back, at least until the quarter ends, which will be the end of summer. I have finals to give," she apologized lamely, hoping he would understand her commitment.

"Sloan," Wes reassured her quickly, sensing her distress, "the end of summer will be fine. I can set up an office in your house somewhere and catch up on paperwork. And phone calls. And I can fly in and out for emergencies. Just make sure they know you won't be back for the fall term."

Sloan smiled, astounded that he would so willingly arrange his life-style around hers. "Thank you, Wes," she said softly. "I promise I won't always be this difficult."

He laughed. "I promise I won't always let you be this difficult! Oh — one more thing," he added quickly. "How could I forget. It's about the most important thing!" He handed her a business card. "My attorney," he explained. "I've drawn up adoption papers for the children. I don't want to try to take Terry's place with them, but they can take back his name as adults if they choose. It will be to their benefit to be my legal heirs, insurance and all that. If you have any objection, I'll understand, but I knew we didn't have much time, so I set the wheels turning last night. Hopefully we can get a judgment by Friday." He grinned a little dryly. "Sometimes it helps to be well known."

Sloan suddenly felt as if she were shattering, breaking apart bit by bit. She had been so strong for so long, and now it was all being lifted from her shoulders. She was off-balance with the weight of burden gone, stunned by the depths of caring Wes showed her with his every thought. Tears glazed her eyes, she didn't deserve this wonder that she had schemed and deceived to bring about, but it was hers now, and she would cling tenaciously to it.

"Sloan," Wes began, his brow tight and features tense as he misread her silence. "If you prefer that I don't adopt the kids —"

"Oh, no!" Sloan protested hastily, shaking

her head and squeezing her eyes tightly shut as she fought to weld the pieces of her self-control back together. "I think it's wonderful that you thought of such a thing," she said hastily. "I'll see the lawyer today for sure." She summoned up a sturdy smile. "And I'll get Florence on to the moving, and get George on to selling your house. And" — her voice fell deep and husky — "I'll have everything set for the wedding, and I'll be missing you like crazy until Friday night!"

Their eyes met across the table, Sloan's for once covered by no shields to hide deceit. They were star-glazed and incredulous. . . . She had never known simple feeling and happiness could be so damned good.

A moment later she was kissing him good-bye, clinging to his powerful frame with the real pain of parting. "It will only be a few days, sweetheart," Wes mumbled gently, his face buried in the silkiness of her hair. "Just a few days . . ."

Then he was gone, and Sloan was drifting on a high plateau of clouds. "Just a few days," she repeated to herself, and then she would have her newfound love forever, sanctioned by the laws of God and State. She didn't think it possible to be any happier.

Jim accepted her news with calm and

pleasant resignation. "I admit," he said with a grin, "I didn't expect this all to come about so quickly, but" — he gave her a broad grin — "I wasn't really planning on having you for the fall quarter. You know," he mused, "I might not be here myself."

"Really?" Sloan queried, surprised. "Why not?"

"If I can swing the financing, I'm going to open a school and perhaps form a professional company."

"That's marvelous!" Sloan applauded him. "Maybe you'll let me 'guest' teach when I'm in Gettysburg!"

"There will always be a place open for you, Sloan," he assured her. "Anyway, at this time, it's only talk. . . . So when is the wedding? Saturday, you say? Do I get to be there?"

"Of course." Sloan grinned. "Family and adoptive family. You fit the latter category!"

The children — Jamie being the only one with a coherent memory of his real father — thought the idea of their mother marrying Wes and providing them with a new father was wonderful. They were thrilled that both Florence and Wes would be living with them, enthusiastic about moving to Kentucky where they could keep a pony.

The only person who accepted Sloan's news dubiously was — oddly enough — Cassie. Sloan wasn't sure exactly what went on in her sister's mind; Cassie didn't say much, but that was why Sloan was bothered. Cassie should have been as ecstatic as she — after all, Cassie had practically thrown them together.

Despite her unusual quiet and reserve, Cassie spent the days helping Sloan. She promised to handle all the catering arrangements for the wedding and also handle the details like cleaning, flowers, liquor, etc. George was happy to handle the sale of Wes's house; Wesley's attorney was a pleasant sort who seemed to take everything in stride, as if instant adoptions were a daily thing. He wished her the best of luck, smiling sheepishly as he told her he could well understand his client's rush.

With all that going on, Sloan didn't worry overmuch about her sister. She was determined to take all of her classes each day, since she would be putting such a burden on Jim when she was gone. Along with working, she was busy helping Florence move in and packing the few personal items Wes had in his house. They wouldn't be back in it once the wedding had taken place.

On Thursday morning Cassie called her

at work. "I think you've forgotten something," she advised.

"What?" Sloan asked, frowning into the wire. She'd kept checklists on everything she was doing, and as far as she could tell, things were going fine.

"Shopping. If I'm not mistaken, your wardrobe isn't going to make a European trip."

"Oooooh." Sloan had been standing and she sat. Cassie was right; her wardrobe was practically nonexistent — she had been carefully pulling together her few decent outfits each time she saw Wes.

"I'll pick you up at work," Cassie said. "George can bring the kids to Florence for you, and you and I can have dinner and do a little spending."

Sloan thought for a moment. She had her paycheck in her purse, and now there wasn't any reason why she shouldn't spend it. By habit she hadn't cashed it, mentally balancing mortgage payments and bills. And now, suddenly, what was a huge sum to her was pennies to Wes. She chuckled softly. She could easily spend the entire sum, and Wes would still think her thrifty.

"Thanks, Cass," Sloan said. "Sounds like a good idea."

It wasn't until she set the receiver down that she realized Cassie had sounded funny.

She wasn't really interested in shopping — she was interested in having dinner together and . . . talking?

Maybe she had been wrong, Sloan thought later as she and Cassie both decided on spinach salad at a local restaurant. Cassie was remaining as reserved as she had been about the whole thing. Several times as they chatted she was sure Cassie was going to say something about the problem bothering her, but she didn't. Still, it was odd. They talked about everything but the wedding.

Cassie livened up when Sloan went on her spending spree, giving harsh sibling advice on colors and styles. "This is fun," Cassie commented after helping Sloan put together several outfits that matched from the panties on out. "Buying anything you want . . ." Her voice trailed away. "Negligees!" she interrupted herself with a giggle. "I don't guess you get to wear them long, but that boutique across the street has some stunning pieces!"

Sloan followed her sister with her pile of boxes, frowning. She was ready to stop in the street and demand to know what was wrong, but Cassie was well ahead of her, and then they were surrounded by salespeople. By the time Cassie had made her try

160

on a dozen garments, she was tired, and her sister's peculiar behavior had drifted to the back of her mind. She didn't think of it again until Cassie was dropping her at her car. "Sloan," Cassie began, stopping her as she walked the few feet in the school's parking lot.

Sloan turned back to her, balancing her stack of packages. "Yes."

"Oh . . . never mind." Cassie waved with a weak smile and drove away.

"What is with her?" Sloan mumbled to herself, shrugging as she fumbled to open the car door. When Cassie was ready to say something, Sloan figured, she would. Until then there wasn't much she could do.

At home she displayed everything for Florence's oohs and aahs and sternly told herself to go to bed. Once there, however, she was too nervous and excited to sleep. One more day and Wes would be back, then a single night before the wedding. . . .

She was still nervous when she awoke after her restless night. Knowing that he was coming made her want to see him desperately. Consequently, the day dragged. Classes which usually sped by for her seemed to be interminable. At three o'clock Jim caught her in her office and insisted she go home.

"I can't," Sloan wailed, "I have an intermediate ballet —"

"Which I can handle," he assured her.

"That's not fair to you, Jim," she objected softly.

"Ah, but the world isn't fair!" Jim chuckled. "Go home. You're driving me insane, and the students may never be the same again. They're limping around as if they've been working out for the Olympics! They aren't all floating on clouds of ecstasy, you know."

Sloan blushed. "I guess I did drive them pretty hard," Sloan murmured.

"That's okay." Jim chuckled. "It's good for them. But do us all a favor and go home! What time is Wes coming in?"

"I don't know," Sloan replied with a sigh. "But since you're being so magnanimous, I guess I will go home. Thanks, Jim."

"Thank you," he told her seriously. "I'm glad you're coming back to finish the quarter."

Sloan shrugged. "I like teaching," she murmured. "I like the students, and, well, I certainly owe you that much!"

"You owe yourself, Sloan, and you owe Wes," Jim advised softly. "Remember that. Now —" He stared at her sternly. "Get out!"

"Okay, okay!" Sloan laughed. "I'll get everything going smoothly!"

Her shower went smoothly; that was all that did. She burned dinner, knocked her iced tea all over the table, and put Terry's sleeper on inside out. After she stubbed her toe viciously while pacing the living room. Florence finally spoke up in the stern voice she used occasionally on the children.

"Settle down, young lady," she commanded. "You're wearing yourself to a frazzle. You'll be a pathetic-looking bride in the morning if you keep this up! Wesley *will* get here, but you can't make him get here any faster by chewing off your manicure."

Wincing while she held her toe, Sloan had to agree. "I think I'll fix myself a scotch and see what's on TV."

"That's a good idea. I'll even join you!"

Florence kept up a stream of chatter as they sat over scotches, tactfully keeping Sloan's mind busy. They slowly went over all of the arrangements together and arrived at the conclusion that nothing had been forgotten. Then, as the eleven o'clock news came on, Sloan caught her new housekeeper friend yawning and winced. She had been so embroiled with her own thoughts that she had given no consideration to Florence!

"Okay, young lady," Sloan said gruffly,

imitating Florence's own tone. "Up to bed with you! You've been a doll! An absolute doll. But I'm fine now, I really am, and I can wait by myself."

Florence was uncertain. "Are you sure?"

"Believe me." Sloan laughed. "I'm calm! Three stiff scotches and I'm not *just* calm — I'm almost out on my feet!"

"All right, then." Florence stifled another yawn and sheepishly admitted she was half-asleep already.

"See you in the morning," she said, kissing Sloan's cheek affectionately. "Give Wes my love and a piece of my mind when he gets in! Although I don't think you'll get much chance to yell at him" — the house-keeper chuckled — "he'll probably just say hi and bye until tomorrow. It is getting dreadfully late, and it will be a full day."

Sloan grinned in return. "I'm not sure yet if I'm going to yell, hit him, or keep my mouth shut and kiss him in relief! Oh!" she asked, concerned for the graying lady who had cheerfully made her own life so much more pleasant with her courtesy, "Shall I turn off the TV? Will the noise disturb you?"

"Don't be silly," Florence protested, shaking her head. "In fact, you could blast it, and the neighbors would know before I did. I'm a heavy sleeper — you've heard my alarm clock. It's worse than a power drill because that's about all that will wake me up." She yawned again. "And all that scotch! My dear, I will probably pass out rather than fall asleep!"

Sloan chuckled. "Well, good. Then I won't worry if I do decide I'm going to yell at Wes."

"Yell away." Florence yawned, moving toward the stairs with a mischievous twinkle in her eyes. "Straighten him out on these late hours of his *before* the wedding!"

It was a good thing, Sloan thought wryly as she watched Florence walk up to bed, that she and Florence had imbibed in the scotches. Her emotions were running the gauntlet — from eager anticipation to anxious worry to frustration and therefore to growing anger. She really might be ready to yell her head off by the time he came in.

What was taking so long? Wes had called on Wednesday night, and everything had been fine. The "farm," as he called it, was running smoothly; his brother and sister-in-law were going to be able to make the wedding. The man had definitely said he'd be in on Friday night.

She was going to have a thing or two to tell him about phoning in the future if he was held up!

"Ummmph!" she said aloud to the clock with disgruntled anger. "He only has forty-five minutes of *Friday* night left!"

Sloan watched the clock for a few more minutes as she listened to the news drone on. With a sigh she despondently sauntered into her bedroom and changed into a slightly worn peignoir set. Her new ones were packed, but if she was going to wind up sleeping in a chair as she fitfully waited, she might as well be dressed comfortably.

Tiptoeing, she checked on the kids and then Florence. Chuckling softly as she reclosed the older woman's door, Sloan had to agree that she slept like death; her soft snores were already deep and steady.

Downstairs, she curled into the sofa before the TV and, turning up the volume, convinced herself that she was going to pay attention to the old Boris Karloff movie coming onto the screen. It was something about a mummy, she realized, yawning with exhaustion herself. Then, somewhere along the line, she drifted into a doze. She awoke ecstatically to see car lights flashing across the walls through the drapes. The sound of tires on gravel assured her she hadn't been dreaming, and she leaped to her feet to throw open the front door with eager relief and an excitement that quickly turned to stunned surprise.

It wasn't Wesley walking up to the house, but Cassie.

Sloan whistled her sister's name in disbelief. "Cassie! What are you doing here? Do you have any idea of what time it is?"

Cassie shrugged, brushing past Sloan. "I came to have a cup of tea with my sister on the night before her wedding."

"Oh, I see," Sloan murmured sardonically, crossing her arms over her chest and following Cassie into the kitchen, still so surprised she forgot to close the door. "Clear as day." Cassie was calmly filling the kettle with water. "That's what you told George," Sloan stated.

"That's what I'm doing, isn't it?" Cassie questioned serenely.

"Precisely," Sloan acknowledged dryly. "Okay, Cass, what is this all about?"

"You have to call off the wedding," Cassie said bluntly, not watching Sloan as she set mugs on the table.

"What?" Sloan shrieked.

"Will you hush up!" Cassie hissed. "You're going to wake your whole house."

Sloan waved a hand in the air impatiently. "No one is going to wake up. The kids have been in bed for hours, and Florence is in another world. Now what in the world are you talking about?"

"You know what I'm talking about," Cassie said miserably. "You can't marry Wes. You're my sister, Sloan, and I love you, but I can't stand by and watch you use a wonderful man like Wes because you'll only make both your lives miserable."

"What do you mean?" Sloan asked thickly.

"You're rushing things, Sloan," Cassie said, her brown eyes deep with unhappy turmoil as she met her sister's gaze squarely. "I've wanted to talk to you all week, but I keep telling myself I'm not your parent, guardian, or conscience. And I'd hoped from the moment I saw Wes and knew he was interested in you that something would form between you." She stopped speaking, bit her lip, and drew a long breath to begin again as Sloan stared at her blankly. "Sloan, I *know* you. I've known you all my life. Even when we were kids, you could charm the pants off of anyone you set your mind to. You were never cruel or malicious, but you could turn on that smile and connive just about anything. I saw you get your way with that sweetly subtle cajolery with Mom and Dad and Terry — and me! And it's not bad, Sloan, it's tactful and polite and no one usu-

168

ally knows he or she has even been taken! I'm sure that sometimes you don't even know you're doing it. But this time I'm sure you do, Sloan," she said gravely. "This time you've turned on the charm for all the wrong reasons! You're marrying Wes for his money."

"Cassie!" Sloan gasped, stunned by her sister's intuitive grasp of her initial motives. "Cassie, you're wrong!" she insisted, but she had never lied to her sister, and the fact that she was right about the original scheming made Sloan's protest weak.

Cassie shook her head, her eyes sad. "You said yes to a proposal in a week, Sloan, to a man you were barely polite to at first."

"Oh, Cassie," Sloan murmured, loving her sister and unable to bear her condemnation. "You *were* right. But not now." The screaming hiss of the teakettle momentarily halted her explanation — and also covered all other sounds in the house. Sloan grabbed the water and poured it over tea bags in the mugs and curled into a kitchen chair before continuing. "Cassie, everything was going to hell! I was overdue on the mortgage, the electricity — everything. So yes, I did set out to charm Wes. I had to get him to marry me; I needed his money."

"Oh, Sloan!" Cassie admonished miserably. "Without love?"

Sloan was fumbling for a way to explain how things had changed. "No, I didn't love him when I knew I had to make it be marriage. I —"

The sharp sound of the front door closing froze Sloan before she could go any further. "Wes!" she exclaimed to Cassie in a quiet hiss. Her sister had taken her so off guard that she had forgotten his expected arrival. "Cassie — I'll finish explaining later," she begged in a whisper, her eyes wide and pleading.

Cassie might attack her on moral grounds when they were alone, but as a sister she was true blue. Her voice rose cheerfully. "Sloan — I think he's finally made it here!"

Both sisters set their mugs down and almost knocked each other over in their guilty haste to reach the living room. "Wesley!" Sloan cried happily as she saw his tall form in the doorway. She raced across the room to embrace him, unaware in her own exuberance that he accepted her stiffly.

"You're late!" Cassie teased from her distance. "I'd better get on home so that you two can have your words out!"

Wes brushed Sloan's forehead with a kiss and smiled at Cassie. "No, Cass, don't leave on my account. I did run late, so I'm just stopping by to say that I'm here."

"Stopping by?" Sloan questioned him with a frown. She blushed slightly, not sure how to phrase her confusion with Cassie present. "Wes, your things are all here. Florence and I cleared out your house except for the things we'll need for the wedding. I — I thought you'd stay here tonight," she stammered.

Wes slipped an arm around her and tilted her chin. He smiled, but she noticed how hard the angles of his face could be, how tense the bronzed skin that stretched across them. He was tired, she realized, very tired. His eyes also had a peculiar light, one that glittered icily in the dim light of the doorway. "I wouldn't dream of staying here tonight," he teased, his voice husky. "We want to get that wedding ring on your finger, my love, and they say it's bad luck for the groom to see the bride before the wedding. I don't think we'll be needing any bad luck, do you?"

"No, of course not," Sloan agreed slowly, the chill his eyes had given her dissipated by the intense heat radiating from his body. Actually, she didn't give a damn about bad luck; he was here, and she wanted nothing more than to stay in his arms and quell the terrible aching she felt for him to hold her, to kiss her, to touch her. . . . "It's just that I've missed you so!" she whispered, loath to release him.

"Listen, I really am going —" Cassie began.

"No, no," Wes protested with firm haste. "I haven't had any sleep, and I think I'm going to need some to deal with my charming bride." He turned to Sloan, the smooth curve of his lip forming a smile that didn't reach his eyes. "Kiss me quick, love. I think I'd better get out of here" — his smile broadened, but there was a dry twist to his words — "before I lose my control with you completely, Sloan."

Sloan laughed, unaware that there could be a double meaning to his words. She kissed him, relishing the commanding feel of his lips upon hers, sensing something warm and combustible in his restrained passion. Tomorrow, she told herself, reluctantly allowing him to pull back from their embrace. Less than ten hours would see them man and wife. . . .

"You should have called," she chastised him huskily. "I was worried."

"Were you?" His grip on her shoulders was strong, almost painful; his kiss had been bruising. Neither bothered Sloan. He had missed her as much as she had missed him.

"Yes, of course," he murmured. "The wedding isn't until tomorrow."

Sloan frowned. "I know, but you said you'd be in tonight —"

"I am going!" Cassie interrupted.

"No, I am!" Wes chuckled, pulling Sloan to him once more so that she felt the thunderous pounding of his heart. He pulled away just as abruptly. "Cassie — goodnight. Sloan. . . ." He ran a finger along her cheek, a tender movement that became tense. "Tomorrow, love." He turned and exited before she could make another protest or chastisement.

Both sisters were silent for several seconds, Sloan mainly because she felt the sun had warmed her only to be covered by a cloud, Cassie because she was relieved that they had heard the door and hushed their conversation. She finally cleared her throat, wondering if Sloan, who was still staring at the door with brilliant, longing eyes, remembered that she was there.

Sloan spun around to face her. "Cassie!" She chuckled, running to hug her sister. "Don't you see? Everything is all right! I did set out to use Wes, but I did fall in love with him! Hopelessly. Completely. If he didn't have a penny to his name, I would feel the same way about him. He's wonderful and —

oh, just everything! I think I'm the luckiest woman in the world!"

Cassie breathed a sigh of happy relief. "I believe you," she said sheepishly. "No woman who isn't in love can carry stars in her eyes like you are now. I'm all for you, sis — I wish you both the best of everything. And I'm going home now, with a nice clear conscience. George already thinks I'm crazy for streaking out of the house in the middle of the night like this. Go get some sleep, kid! You'll be a bride in the morning."

The sisters hugged again, and Sloan watched until her sister was safely in the car. Then she locked the door and waltzed into her room.

She slept easily, ecstatic that Wes was back, and even if he wasn't with her that night, there would never have to be another night when he wasn't. She dreamed of her wonderful luck.

# CHAPTER SEVEN

Sloan didn't see Wesley again until the ceremony, which was, according to their desires, simple but beautiful. Fragrant displays of summer flowers were the only decoration; the lilting strains of a single guitar the only music. Cassie acted as matron of honor, Wesley's brother Dave as best man. Sloan, in a cloud of excitement and euphoria, barely heard the words spoken, and although Wes's replies were strong and sure, she had to be nudged by Cassie to speak at the appropriate times.

Then the brief ceremony was over; they were officially man and wife. Wesley bent obediently to kiss her; and as his lips claimed hers, Sloan felt a tension and hint of punishment in the pressure of his arms.

It's the time we've been apart, she thought with loving tolerance. He released her, and their eyes met. For a second it seemed as if Wesley stared at her with cold, fathomless disdain. Then the look was gone, and she dismissed it from her mind as fancy. She was smiling up at *Wes,* handsome and as benevolent as an ancient god in the formfitting tux and exquisite laced shirt which seemed but to enhance every majestic line of his masculinity. Sloan reeled with the impact of his return smile, drunk from his aura and presence. She felt like Sleeping Beauty; awoken by a kiss only to find the real prince of her dreams. Was it a dream? she wondered blissfully. It was all too good to be true. Or did every bride feel the way that she did at the moment, even if it was the second time around?

The reception passed in as much of a blur as the wedding. Wes's brother and sister-in-law were an attractive, charming couple; Dave was a slimmer version of his brother and every bit as personable; Susan, a vivacious, down-to-earth woman Sloan immediately liked. The children pranced about gleefully, delighted to be participating in grown-up affairs, stealing sips of champagne from any available glass that fell their way. Before she knew it, Sloan, higher than ever on her cloud after several glasses of the delicious champagne, was being ushered into Wes's room to change for her honeymoon.

"Oh, Sloan!" Cassie marveled breathlessly as she followed her sister into the room and closed the door behind her. Tears of happiness formed in her deep brown eyes. "You're so beautiful today, so radiant! I'm so happy for you." Flying across the room, she embraced Sloan with a strangling hug.

"Thanks, Cassie," Sloan whispered. Then they were laughing and crying together, and Sloan's dress was spotted by their joyous tears.

Cassie finally extracted herself and smiled at Sloan from arm's distance. "I'm going to miss you. . . ."

"I won't be gone long, and I'll deluge you with postcards —"

"That's not what I mean," Cassie said, choking on a sniffle. "You'll be gone for good when you get back."

"Not for good!" Sloan protested, feeling nostalgic pangs of departure herself but determined to cheer Cassie. "We'll be living in Gettysburg part time!"

"Yeah," Cassie agreed, forcing a smile. "What am I doing?" she moaned. "I'm not supposed to be making you weepy on your wedding day!"

"Zip my zipper then," Sloan directed. "We've a long ride to the airport."

Sloan's travel outfit was a tailored, powder-blue dress with a matching jacket for the sound possibility of cooler weather when their plane landed in Belgium. The sisters chatted as Sloan retouched her makeup and unnecessarily straightened her clothing for a last time. "I'm ready, I guess," Sloan finally said.

"You sound reluctant," Cassie laughed. "Nervous?"

"Yep."

"Goodness — why?" Cassie demanded.

Sloan had to stop and think. "I don't know. Aren't all brides nervous?"

"To a point," Cassie agreed. "But not all brides get to marry Wes! He's the nicest man . . . always so calm and gentle! I'd trust him with my life and —" Cassie broke off, blushing.

"And what?"

"I'll bet he's a hell of a lover!"

Sloan started to giggle. "I'll bet you're right!"

Just then Laura came racing into the room, tears flooding down her little cheeks. Sloan scooped her daughter into her arms. "Darling! What's the matter?"

It was difficult to understand Laura's garbled sobbings, but Sloan eventually deciphered the cause for her daughter's misery; Laura had just realized that her mother was actually leaving her for two weeks.

Crooning into Laura's silky-soft hair, Sloan assured her that she wouldn't be gone long and that Florence and Cassie would take good care of her. Laura continued to cry.

"What's the problem?"

Sloan looked up to find Wesley leaning in the doorframe. Raising her hands helplessly, she explained, "Laura doesn't want us to go."

Without another word to Sloan, Wes took the little girl from her arms. In a soothing voice, but one which he might also use on an adult, Wesley patiently told her that they were going on a honeymoon, and people usually did when they were married. He promised sincerely that they wouldn't be gone long and that they would send post-cards and bring home special presents for everyone. Laura's sniffles slowly subsided, and before long she was asking Wesley to make sure he brought her a doll. She was all smiles by the time he set her down, eager to kiss them both good-bye.

Sloan and Wes had no further problems leaving. Jamie told them good-bye and to have a great time in a very adult manner; Terry was happily crunching crackers his aunt had given him and barely brushed his

179

mother with a gritty kiss. To the happy strains of laughter and a shower of rice, Wes led his new bride to the car.

Sloan's nervousness increased as Wesley silently drove. Unaccountably, she was becoming terribly uneasy in his company. Remembering her sister's words, she tried to settle comfortably into her seat. Wes was a terrific man, always calm and understanding. And he would be, she was sure as a thrill of heat raced through her at the thought, a superb lover. If "previews" meant anything . . . Yet even as she deliciously contemplated the night, a vision of the icy hardness of his eyes as he stared at her after the ceremony rose unbidden to her mind. Stop! she warned herself. She could relax now, feel young.

Sitting up abruptly, she shook her head as if to clear it and turned to her new husband with a smile. Her wanderings were absurd and ridiculous! She knew Wes, she loved and understood him completely. He was the nicest, most wonderful man in the world, and any suspicions to the contrary were pure imagination on her part! They loved one another, and love was comfortable, secure . . . fun! She had invented his look of this morning in her mind; it had been a trick of light.

Resting her hand lightly on his thigh, she said, "Thanks for handling Laura so well. She was breaking my heart."

Wes shrugged, his eyes planted squarely on the road. "I'm crazy about the kids, you know that. And they're not your children anymore; they're *ours*."

"I love you," Sloan said softly.

"Do you?"

Whatever reply Sloan had been expecting, that wasn't it. She studied him, puzzled. "You know I love you," she said, hurt. "Why else . . ."

Wesley's arm came around her neck, and he ruffled the hair at its nape. "We all like assurance," he said, and he glanced at her quickly. His eyes were full of their sea-jade warmth, and Sloan relaxed. Everything was all right.

"Why don't you settle down for a bit of a nap," Wes suggested, idly stroking her hair. "We've still got quite a drive to the airport, then a long flight, and it will be morning all over again when we land. Might be some time before we get to bed, and then —" He juggled his eyebrows insinuatively, and Sloan blushed like a girl and chuckled.

"Well, hell!" he grumbled with a wink. "One of us is going to need a lot of energy!"

"Okay, okay," Sloan retorted, stretching

across the car and resting her head in his lap. "I'm napping!"

After the excitement of boarding the plane and moving out over the Atlantic had also diminished, Sloan again cuddled into her reclining chair, her hand resting possessively in Wesley's, and slipped into another catnap. It was easy to sleep with the clouds out her window and the faint hum of the engines lulling in her ears. So easy, in fact, that Wesley was shaking her awake before she could believe the long flight had passed.

An hour later they were standing in the middle of Brussels' magnificent Grand Place while her citizens busily scurried about. Sloan stared in awe at the breathtaking visage of the city center. The buildings, though grayed and sooted with age, were spectacular. In the brilliance of the summer sun, they shone like a fairy tale, all white and glittering gold and carved with exquisite artistry.

"We'll just walk around a little and get the feel of the city," Wes said, taking her arm. "Feast on a delectable meal of French cuisine and head out for the hotel. Tomorrow we can start sightseeing."

"Tomorrow," Sloan laughed. "It is tomorrow."

"Not here." Wes grinned.

Wes pointed out certain of the gold-gilded buildings as they walked, reading from a tourist manual. The city was founded in the 500's, and many of the structures still standing dated back to the 1200's. They viewed with wonder and excitement the old Hotel de Ville, the Church of Saint Gudule, and the more modern Palace of Justice.

"I know it's here somewhere!" Wesley suddenly muttered, his eyes roaming studiously around the market square. "Off the Grand Place . . ."

"What?" Sloan asked curiously, following his line of vision. All she could see was the beautiful square, the bustling people, and a sky full of careless gray pigeons.

"The Kissing Fountain."

"The what?"

Wesley smiled roguishly and set his arm around her waist. "I swear to you, it's one of the 'must sees' in Brussels. Well, it's semi-famous. Among honeymooners, anyway."

Sloan raised a brow. "Because the fountain kisses?"

"That's right."

"I don't believe you."

"Well, it's true," Wesley promised solemnly. "And do you know how?"

Sloan stared at him skeptically. "Somehow with water, I assume."

"You got it!" Wes grinned. "Come on, let's find it."

Laughing happily in the comfort of her husband's arm, Sloan ambled along the street with him. She was in for her first surprise when Wesley stopped a passerby and asked what she assumed were directions in what sounded like perfect French.

"It's on a side street off the Grand Place," Wes explained, without blinking an eye after he had been answered. "Follow, my love, and I shan't lead you astray."

"You never told me you spoke French," Sloan said reproachfully.

"You never asked."

Sloan smiled. "I guess we'll make surprising discoveries every day."

"Ummm . . ." Wes stared down at her, and for a fraction of a minute she thought she caught that strange coldness in his eyes again. Then it was gone, and he hugged her to him. "Discoveries are amazing, love. In fact, my darling, you never fail to amaze and surprise me. . . ."

After a few wrong turns, they came upon the "famous" Kissing Fountain, and like teenaged lovers they fell into one another's arms with uproarious laughter. Privately owned, the fountain was a tiny thing, composed of a chubby little girl and an equally chubby little boy, gilded beautifully in Brussels gold. As the water pressure rose from the ground, the pair turned to one another and "kissed," then swiveled again in their elegant garden with pretty pursed lips — to spout a misting flood of water upon any audience.

"This is a 'must see,' huh?" Sloan demanded, giggling as she wiped water from her cheeks. "I'll bet it's not listed in the majority of the tourist manuals!"

"Hey! What do you want?" Wes retorted good-naturedly. "Some world traveler you make! I told you, this is one of the things one does in Brussels!" His arm tightened around her waist, and he pulled her closely to him. "But now that we've done it . . ." His voice was low and husky. "Now we'll go for that French meal and head for our romantic room. . . ."

The restaurant Wes chose was right on the Grand Place, and they were quickly ushered to a discreet table which still allowed for a marvelous view of the quaint glittering buildings. The daytime light was muted to mellow the room and necessitate the use of a single, mood-setting candle at each table. Garlands of roses highlighted the intricately carved, heavy wood furnishings and contrasted with the velvety black booths. Sloan sank into the comfort of the booth gratefully and relished in the delight of Wes's hard body against hers. She acquiesced with a pretty grin when he suggested he order for them both and gave herself completely to the elegantly romantic mood surrounding them. It was so nice! So easy to rest against the sure shoulder beside her and put herself into the hands of the man she loved with no doubts or second thoughts.

"Well, darling" — Wesley turned to her and raised his glass when they had been served a delicious, dry white wine — "to that ring upon your finger." In the candlelight, he had a decidedly rakish expression, like that of a pirate, smiling with secret triumph as he gloated over his gold. It was odd that the wavering shadows of the candle could cause such an effect; Wes appeared almost scary but, Sloan thought as a warm shiver of anticipation bubbled in her veins, oh, so sexy!

"To us!" she corrected, raising her glass to tip to his. "That gold thing on your finger is a wedding band, too."

"Ummm . . ." But Wes's mind wasn't on his own finger or the gold band that adorned it. He was watching Sloan with his pirate expression, his eyes now as brilliant as the gilded buildings outside. With his left hand he held his wineglass; with his right hand he stroked her cheek in a feathery light caress. His thumb rubbed her lips with a tantalizing combination of roughness and care, persisting until she smiled and returned the sensual taunt by grazing her teeth over the thumb. "Ummmm . . ." Wesley repeated. "And I ordered escargot. You, my love, are all the appetizer, entree, and dessert I think I really require at the moment —"

"I thought you were starving," Sloan interrupted.

"Oh, I am," Wes retorted, brushing her lips with a kiss. But the arrival of their escargots — aromatic with subtle seasonings and dripping in a delicious butter sauce — curtailed any explanation of just what he was starving for.

The escargots were followed by an untouchable onion soup baked with a blend of cheeses and toasted cubes of French bread to perfection. Sloan moaned at the arrival of their main course, delicately seasoned fish, swearing she would never be able to finish the food. She did, however; it was all too delicious to consider leaving a mouthful.

Sloan demurred on dessert, but agreed to join Wes in ordering coffee and Grand

Marnier. Twilight was falling as they sipped their cordials, and the muted blendings of gold and crimson added to the mystical romance of the evening. Sloan was marvelously comfortable and at ease. The liquor she had consumed made her feel as if she were truly floating on clouds, her body as light as a feather but superbly attuned to the touch and feel of the man beside her — the man who was now her husband and would soon be claiming all of his matrimonial rights. The thought made her shudder with delicious anticipation, and yet she was willing to savor every minute, to let things follow their dreamlike path slowly so that each step on the way to ultimate fulfillment could be cherished and heighten all that was to come. . . .

She was almost in a trance by the time Wesley reached for her hand and escorted her from the restaurant. He was strangely silent as he guided their rental car out of the center of the city and into the surrounding hills, but Sloan barely noticed. Her head was resting on his shoulder; her hand rested lightly on his thigh, and she was secretly thrilling to its rugged, tense feel beneath her fingers. His breathing, she noted with misty satisfaction, was growing ragged, and a pulse was visibly pounding in the length of his corded neck. A smile of pure feminine pleasure fitted its way seductively into her lips. Wesley had power over her — he could prove that at any time with the slightest touch! — but she also had power over him, and she knew it. She loved him, desperately, but something as old as love and even more primitive held her in its grasp. Tonight she would play the seductress for real; the sensual vixen to the hilt. In the most ancient of feminine games, she would wield her power with subtle mastery until she had driven Wesley to the brink of insanity. Then, of course, they would surrender to love's sweet fire together. Still, she decided with the wiles of her sex, she would keep the upper hand. It would never do to let Wes know that he could be the eternal victor, while still the game was for them both . . . two winners.

She almost forgot her game when they arrived at their hotel. As Wes had promised, the place was secluded and enchanting. The old and new were blended together delightfully. Their room, furnished with French provincial pieces — the dominating one being a huge, four-poster bed — was also equipped with ultra-modern conveniences. There was nothing outdated about the beautiful marble bath or the plate glass windows which overlooked lush green hills and a blue stream. Flemish tapestries lined the walls, enhancing rather than contrasting with a thick shag rug of creamery-pure beige. Sloan clapped her hands with delight at her surroundings and spun on Wes with the enthusiasm of a child shining her eyes to brilliant sapphire.

"Wes!" she cried happily, lifting her hands inadequately as she sought for words of description. "It's beautiful — wonderful — marvelous!"

A smile tilted his lips, but he turned from her wordlessly to tip the boy who had brought their luggage in. The two exchanged a few words in French, then the boy left, grinning deftly as he pocketed Wes's francs. Then the door closed behind him, and Sloan was at long last alone with her new husband.

Wesley came behind her at the window. Darkness was enveloping the land, but a full moon was steadily rising to cast beautiful, luminescent shadows over the rippling water and nearby foliage. As they stared upon the view together, Wesley's hands spanned her small waist, and he began a series of erotic nibblings on her earlobe which surely found their way down her neck and collarbone. Then he was firmly turning her from the window, and his lips found hers with insistent demand.

Sloan moaned as her lips parted beneath his assault. His tongue plundered the recesses of her mouth mercilessly as his hands began a slow attack of their own. Instinctively Sloan responded, arching her body to his, running her fingers from the crispness of his hair to the strength of his back, luxuriating in the play of muscles beneath her fingertips even as his heat began to consume her. His fingers found the zipper of her dress, and as she heard the rasping sound of its release, she remembered, somewhat vaguely, her game. As his callused hands found her bare flesh and began a possessive exploration, Sloan gently maneuvered from his arms. Having artfully escaped, she smiled at his look of frustrated confusion. Moving quickly before he could reclaim her, she impishly planted a kiss on his chin and sprang from his reach. "I'm going to take a quick shower, darling," she murmured. "I won't be long."

But she was. She allowed the hot water to run on and on, lathering herself richly with scented soap, her lips curled all the while as she gloated over the excitement of her taunting. Finally, she rinsed herself thoroughly and emerged, chuckling in her throat

191

as she noticed the knob of the door twisting. She wasn't ready yet. Taking her time, she assiduously brushed her hair until it fell in silklike waves, then donned one of her new gowns, a deceptive piece of black gauze which covered her from neck to toe yet teased enticingly with slits that ran all the way to her hips. She continued chuckling as she stepped into a pair of black string bikini panties and completed her outfit with the matching black pegnoir. Then she reached for the doorknob, her heart beginning to flutter tremulously.

Wesley was not panting by the door as she had expected. He had discarded his own clothing for a velour robe and was leaning nonchalantly on the bed, one arm behind his head to form a comfortable crook for it, the other resting on his kneecap as he held an iced drink. He had turned on the television set and was watching a newscaster. "I ordered you a scotch," he said, idly motioning toward the dresser. He barely glanced her way.

"Thanks," Sloan said, bewildered. She walked slowly for her drink, swaying as she did so, but she received no response from Wesley. Frustrated, she sipped the scotch and sat at the foot of the bed. If he was giving no notice of her, she certainly wasn't going to jump into his arms! The voice of the newscaster droned into her ears. "That isn't French he's speaking," she said, growing increasingly nervous.

"Flemish," Wes supplied conversationally. "This is bilingual country."

"Oh," Sloan murmured. Then acidly, "And I suppose you speak Flemish, too?"

"Not really," Wes said absently. "I understand a fair amount."

Sloan heard the clatter of ice as Wesley calmly drained his glass. Still, he didn't move. So! Sloan thought petulantly, he wants to play games, too! Well, she had already decided on winning this one. She drained her scotch in a gulp and winced as the burning liquid made its way down her throat. Then she stood, stretched and yawned, surprised at how dizzy she was. Gulping the scotch had been a mistake. Clutching the bedpost, she steadied herself and stole a glance at Wesley. The black hair on his chest curled provocatively over its expanse as it lay exposed from the V of his robe. The knotted muscles of his calves, thrown so carelessly over the coverlet, gave a breath-catching hint of the physique beneath the draped velour. . . .

Damn him! Sloan thought. She whirled from the bedpost and ripped the covers from her side of the bed. She was squirming with heat and anger. It had never occurred to her that two could play her game. . . .

Flouncing into the bed, she turned her back on him and stared at the bathroom door, fuming. His ensuing chuckle, deep, low, and from the throat, was the finishing touch. She determined furiously that whatever the cost to herself, Wesley would go to sleep on his wedding night with nothing more fulfilling than a hot shower!

His hand wrapped around her arm like a vise, and his next whisper was hot and tantalizing against her ear. "No games, my darling," he murmured, his lips moving along her neck and shoulder, searing her skin through the gauze. "You're my wife now. Legal possession."

"Possession!" Sloan shrilled, spinning around so quickly that her hair neatly slapped his face and momentarily curtailed his kisses. The evening was not going at all as planned! Wesley was calm and sedate, taking his own sweet time, and she was a bundle of nerves and frustration. He was supposed to realize she was elated, yet ever so slightly frightened despite her stance, needing him to cajole. Instead, he was calmly telling her that she was a *possession*.

"Ummm," Wes drawled lazily, his nibbling kisses moving over her breasts, warm and moist over the black material. "That's what you are now, you know, a possession."

"No!" Sloan squealed breathlessly. Her fury was mingling with her desire and the undeniable arousal he was so easily eliciting. Mind and body waged a silent war. She had to stop him before it was too late, before she lost herself in the steadily increasing vortex of pleasure he was confidently creating. Her fingers dug into his hair, and she pulled his face to hers with all the strength her anger could muster.

"Ouch!" he exclaimed, and then she saw his eyes and the amusement that sparkled within them.

"You've been teasing me!" Sloan accused, relaxing somewhat but maintaining her punishing grasp of his hair. "You . . . you . . . you . . ." She couldn't think of a fit name to call him.

"How about 'Lord and Master,' " Wes taunted, placidly circling her wrists with his hands and creating a pressure which forced her to gasp and release her hold. Then both of her wrists were firmly held by one of his hands and pinioned above her.

" 'Lord and Master' my foot!" Sloan retorted, squirming and wriggling her wrists to free herself. The effort was ludicrous.

"I'll get you for this, Wesley Adams," she said tartly, panting but unwilling to accept defeat.

"I do hope that's a promise," he drawled languorously. "Now," he continued, his tone lowering hoarsely, "just how do you plan to get me? Like this?" She felt the rough fingertips of his free hand delve beneath the black gown to travel with tantalizing leisure up the length of her thigh. "Or perhaps like this." With a force belying his subtle tone, he deftly drove a wedge between her legs with a firm thrust of a knee and lowered his weight over her body, imprisoning her completely.

"Wesley!" Sloan's calling of his name was a combination of amazement, irritation, amusement and — despite her firm resolve to remain unmoved by any of his advances until she was in control again — exquisite pleasure.

"Maybe you could 'get me' something like this," he went on, undaunted. He showered her throat and breasts again with the moist, nibbled kisses that were driving all rational thoughts from her mind as they ignited a fire within her that raged rapidly to every tingling nerve of her body. "Maybe more like this," he muttered darkly against her skin, and then before she knew his purpose, his teeth sank into the material of her gown as his hand momentarily halted its wanderings to rip the black gauze cleanly in two, leaving her slender form bared to his sensuous view. "What the hell are these things?" he demanded, slipping a finger beneath the elastic of the black panties. "Oh well, what the hell." A single twist of his fingers ripped the string, and he tossed them to the floor with a nonchalant flick of his hand.

"Wesley!" Sloan gasped again. The word was meant to sound indignant, reproachful, but his name came out instead as a groaning plea. "Stop it!" she murmured weakly, renewing the struggle for freedom of her hands.

"Stop what?" he teased. "This?" His fingers began a feather-light caress on her belly, drawing circles that became larger and more inquisitive as he shifted slightly and continued to the sensitive silk of her thighs. "Or this . . ." His voice grated on the last, and the hands and fingers that sought the secrets of her femininity were no longer fluttery and teasing but hungry and demanding as was the mouth that claimed her breasts, arousing them to rigid peaks.

Sloan shivered uncontrollably, writhing and squirming, but no longer to escape his hold. She wanted to get closer to him, closer and closer, become one with him and allow the fire that now pulsed through her like a living thing to burn to its height of shimmering flame and ultimately consume them.

"Wildcat," Wesley murmured to the roseate nipple his lips caressed. His face rose above Sloan's, and she was dimly aware that his eyes glittered like a jungle cat's and that his features were taut with his own desire. "My game, now, wife, and then no more games," he muttered darkly.

"No more games," Sloan echoed in a husky whisper, shuddering as if charged by electricity and arching to feel the crisp hairs of his chest against her breasts and the pulsating hardness of his masculinity that blatantly proved his own arousal. "Wesley . . . please!" Her words were almost a sob.

But he wasn't through with his exquisite torture yet. He released her wrists, but only to allow his lips further exploration of her flesh. Freed, Sloan's hands moved of their own volition, clinging to him, digging into him, seeking and desiring. And then, when she thought she would surely die of wonderful agony, Wesley's hands moved to her buttocks and lifted her to him.

"Surrender?" He was gloating, but his demand was uttered in such a raw rasp that it didn't matter. It didn't matter anyway. He had driven her to an absolute frenzy.

"Surrender," she croaked, parting her lips and hooking her arms desperately around the hard expanse of his shoulders. "No more games. . . ."

Skyrockets of dizzying ecstasy exploded throughout her as Wesley completed his conquest, taking her with a rough urgency that matched the wild passion flaming hungrily between them. Wesley's pulsating rhythm took them higher and higher to peak after peak, bringing them finally to a boundless precipice of sweet satiation that was so wonderful that Sloan could not move at its conclusion, could not disentangle her limbs from Wesley's nor willingly draw away from his overwhelming heat.

It was he who finally moved, but only to shed the robe that still encased his shoulders. He tugged at the remnants of Sloan's black gown. "Get rid of that," he commanded softly.

There was no more fight left in Sloan, just loving, dazed obedience. She knew she had lost the upper hand — if she had ever had it! But she didn't care. Her body still burned with the aftermath of pleasure; the memory of Wesley's demanding possession still throbbed divinely where his virility had split her asunder. Filled with loving contentment, she dutifully cast aside the remainders of the black gauze and curled to his naked side, reveling in the feel of his lean, sinewed body. A sigh of sheer peace and satisfaction escaped her as her eyelids fluttered closed.

"Sleepy?" Wesley queried with a throaty chuckle, stroking her damp hair from her forehead.

"Ummm . . ."

"What? On your honeymoon?" he mocked. "My passionate little wildcat giving out already? Un-unh!"

"Wes," Sloan protested drowsily. "I'm half-asleep . . ."

"I'll wake you up," he promised, and proceeded to prove he could do so. Slowly, more gently this time, with Sloan able to return every spark of arousal and explore him with equal intimacy. He demanded things of her, coaxing her with enticing whispers to tell him everything that pleased her most and exciting her to almost unendurable lengths by encouraging her own shy administrations with hoarse groans and gutteral exclamations of her perfection.

"I think I married a sex maniac," she told him euphorically as he swept her to his heights again.

"No, darling," he muttered, his face taut

with desire, "*I* did, little wildcat."

"I never knew it could be this way. . . ." Anything else she had to say became incomprehensible as moans obliterated her speech.

Later, countless eons later, she drifted off to sleep in the ageless, dreamlike satisfaction of one filled to the brim with enchanted satiation, held in the security of her lover's arms. The night had been more than she had ever expected, even in her wildest imaginings. She had given herself to Wesley completely, and learned the superb sweetness of surrender. It was good, so wonderfully good, to be his and know that he was hers and that a man like Wesley slept beside her. She had been conquered, but the thought bothered her not at all. She didn't need a superior edge anymore; she loved and trusted him totally.

She awoke in the middle of the night, keenly attuned to his touch. She was coiled against him, her back fitted into the curve of his stomach, sheltered by his arms. For a minute she was confused, wondering why she had woken. Then she realized that he was insistently fondling her breasts; the pressure of his powerful chest and his hot, probing masculinity telling her the rest.

"Wes!" she murmured with awe and surprise, a remnant of guile prompting her protest. A laugh escaped her. "We have tomorrow, you know."

"Never put off till tomorrow," he quoted as his teeth grazed her earlobe. Had she been more awake, she might have noticed the slight hesitance before his teasing statement. As it was, she merely mocked a sigh of resignation and succumbed to his advances, shocked by the vehemence of her response and the wild abandon with which she eagerly returned his lovemaking when by all rights she should have been exhausted, spent, and still sound asleep.

Wesley chuckled softly when she shuddered in his arms again. "Go back to sleep, darling," he whispered. "I promise I won't wake you again."

Sloan obligingly rested her head upon his chest. A thought nagged at her, but she was so tired, she couldn't quite put a finger on it. Then it hit her, but by then she was caught in the twilight between sleep and consciousness and she dismissed it immediately.

In all his words of coaxing and passionate encouragement, in all his whispers of hungry pleasure, never once had Wesley said he loved her.

What a ridiculous thing to be thinking about, Sloan thought dimly in her subconscious. She knew Wesley loved her; he had told her so many times, even when she had been setting her "trap" and was totally unaware of her own, intense feelings for him.

And so she slept again, soundly and perfectly happy in her newly discovered joy and fulfillment, blissfully unaware of what the morning would bring.

# CHAPTER EIGHT

The bright, beguiling sunlight of the Belgian morning streaked through the parted drapes to awaken her. Like a purring kitten she stretched languorously; like an innocent maid who had just discovered the wonder of love she flicked shy lashes and reached a tentative hand across the covers to touch her new husband.

He wasn't there. Her eyes opened fully, and she smiled a sweet smile of contentment as she found him, sitting on a bedside chair, his strong fingers idly stroking his chin as he watched her. His dark hair was tousled, his broad chest incredibly sexy in its partial exposure at the loose V of his haphazardly belted robe.

But he didn't smile back, and Sloan's happily curved lips straightened tremulously. His look was as cold as ice, his piercing green eyes brutal in his tense, bronzed face.

Barely awake, Sloan blinked with confusion. It couldn't be Wesley staring at her that way! She opened her eyes again to find the glacial image still before her. She struggled inwardly to ease her bewilderment. What had happened to change the tender and gentle man she had married into this basilisk of condemnation? How could he possibly be staring at her with such venom after the night of passionate love they had just shared together?

"So you're awake."

His voice was low, pleasant, the tone almost silky. For the briefest moment, Sloan began to relax, convincing herself she was reading things into his pirate gaze that simply weren't there.

Then he began to speak again.

"It was . . . interesting? . . . my love, to see how you would handle the night. Very nice. I must say, darling, that when you sell out, you do go all the way with gusto."

A creeping cold chill of fear seeped rapidly through her numbed senses. "What?" she whispered incredulously, moistening dry lips.

"The act is charming, Sloan, but no good." He flashed her a pearly smile with a rapier edge. "It's time for a little honesty."

Lord, she wondered desperately, what *had* happened? "I don't know what you're talking about!" she hedged, panicked. Forcing herself to keep a mask of calm on her features, she thought rapidly over the past events. He couldn't have any suspicions regarding her original motives for marriage; he would have certainly called off the wedding! He *couldn't* know anything harmful, she decided with a quaking bravado. Still, she clutched the covers protectively to her chin as she attempted a captivating grin and laughed gaily. "Really, darling, you should have warned me that you wake like a growling bear!"

Dark brows rose in an arch. "Should I have?" he inquired politely, the daggerlike smile still etched clearly into his taut profile. He stood and sauntered slowly to her while she watched him uneasily. She had the terrible, uncanny feeling that he was playing with her, as a great cat played with its prey before pouncing for the final kill. Her instinct was to run, but she was stubbornly insisting to herself that there was nothing that could be really wrong. Willpower alone kept her still, presenting a facade of guileless calm.

She felt his heat as he sat beside her, felt the tense, powerful coil of his thigh muscle against hers. She forced herself to meet his steel, green gaze unblinkingly, and when his fingers moved gently along her cheekbones and down to her throat, she silently prayed she would not flinch beneath the harsh rigidity that lurked, like a spiral about to spring, behind the tenderness of the gesture. Then she couldn't bear the tense, pregnant stillness any longer. "What is it, love?" she whispered.

"What is it . . . love," he repeated in a toneless, mocking murmur. Then the coil unleashed and the spring flew. His fingers clamped around her wrists like steel cuffs and he jerked her abruptly from the bed. She uttered a startled scream in protest, shocked by his sudden show of ill-controlled force, no longer uneasy or frightened but thoroughly terrified. She was well aware of the bricklike muscles that composed the frame of this man who was now a stranger, well aware that he could break her like so many match sticks if he so desired.

He was oblivious to her cries of protest as he ripped the protective sheet from her and pulled her into the bathroom where he positioned her firmly before the mirror, his hands on her shoulders but warningly near her neck, the breadth of his body behind her, holding her steady as she lowered her eyes and begged him to let her loose.

"Not just yet . . . wife. . . ." he spat, the iciness of his eyes losing nothing as he met the trembling liquid pools of hers in reflection. "We shall see what we have here, first. . . ."

"Wesley!" Sloan implored, stunned by his actions. Wesley Adams couldn't be doing this to her! Even the rough lover of the night before had been tender. . . .

"Now," he continued coldly, ignoring her outburst, his voice that of an informative teacher conducting a class, "what do we have? Do we see a woman approaching thirty, a mother of three, possibly fearful that she may be losing her looks, never again to be loved or cherished? Afraid that she shall not be accepted again by a new lover because of her children? No." One hand slid over her shoulder, cupped a breast, moved on over her rib cage to her flat stomach and harshly molded the jut of her hip. "No," he hissed again, emphatically. "This woman holds no fears. She is serenely confident of her femininity. No naive girl, this. She is a beautiful, bewitching woman, and she knows it. Like a black widow, she can easily lure a man into her web. She is a remarkable animal — breasts full and firm, seductively curved hips, a figure as slim as a debutante's. She doesn't even remember the definition of the word 'love.' "

"Wesley!" Sloan pleaded miserably, shaking with the unexpected vehemence of his mind-boggling attack. "Wesley, please, I beg you!"

"You beg me. Lovely." He laughed dryly, a harsh, bitter, and hollow sound. "Not yet, darling." His hands found her chin and forced her bowed head back to the mirror. "We haven't decided what we do have here, yet. But certainly not a woman clinging to a last line of hope! That I could have understood. Forgiven easily." Her chin jerked cruelly. "Open your eyes!" he commanded.

She obeyed and met orbs of such jade-green loathing that chills exploded violently in spasms throughout her. Still he showed no mercy.

"I have met street prostitutes with more scruples," he continued, his grip like a mechanical thing. "They sell openly, for a price. They make an honest bargain. They tell you what they want, and they tell you exactly what you get in return.

"But you . . . wife . . ." She gasped a choking sob as he spun her around to face him. "You were not honest one stinking step of the way. You lied, connived, cheated, and schemed. You sold yourself more callously than any common tramp. All for my money."

"No!" Sloan protested weakly in self-defense, slowly, sickly realizing he had been in the house at the beginning of her explanation to Cassie, hearing . . .

"Don't lie to me now, woman!" His raging growl bellowed through the room as he shook her so hard that her head lolled like a doll's and her hair fell in torrents over her shoulders. "God, don't try to play me for a fool any longer! Your little game is really up. I heard everything you had to say to your sister, my dear, and though I didn't want to believe it — a man's heart and his ego can be terribly sensitive at times — everything surely fit perfectly. One night you didn't want me crossing your doorstep, the next day you were welcoming me with open arms." He pushed her from him contemptuously. "And I fell for it all! All that false, wide-eyed innocence. I walked into your lair with starry eyes, wanting so desperately to believe in you, respecting your views on sex and marriage when all the while . . ." His voice broke off grimly as he tightly clenched his fist. The lines about his mouth were white with tension. Uttering a croak of disgust, he spun on his heel and stalked from the bathroom.

Sloan stood stock-still for a moment, scarcely breathing, unable to absorb the horror of the things he had said, unable to reconcile them with the man she had known so intimately just hours before. Then she followed him out, nervously grabbed the sheet from the bed to wrap herself in, and skittered into a corner of the room to watch him with dazed, fearful eyes. She had no conception of what he might do next. It was all too evident; the man she thought she knew, understood, the chivalrous wooer, the tenderly possessive lover, existed no more. And she should have never underestimated him. Her vague suspicions that he could be a dangerous man had proved all too true. A tiger, though tamed, was still in essence a wild beast, and Wesley, like that beast, had given up all pretense of civility. Raw instinct and basic fury were guiding him now. Reason and logic had lost all meaning. Like primitive man, he was the stronger, and he would call the shots.

Sloan watched, still too dazed to attempt the explanation he wouldn't believe as he began to pack his bags. Shrunken into her corner, she felt the tears which had formed in her eyes begin to trickle down her cheeks. Whatever happened she knew she deserved, yet how could she lose him now when she had just found him?

His glance fell her way as coolly as marble. "Don't bother with the tears. I'm not going to break your neck, though I should. Nor am I going to annul the marriage, though I should. The children are my responsibility now, too, and there is no reason they should be made to suffer because of their mother."

The tears fell anyway, despite his brutal statements. She couldn't believe the way he was treating her — not after the day and night they had spent happily in one another's arms! "Why? . . ." At first she didn't realize she had said the word aloud.

"What?" Wesley barked.

"Why? . . ." She shrank even further into her corner, unable to complete her question beneath the survey of his relentless anger.

In two seconds he reached her, pulled her to her feet, and swung her gracelessly into the middle of the room. "Why what?" he demanded, his eyes blazing a dancing flame of green fire. "Don't turn coward on top of everything else. You're not the least upset over what you did; selling out didn't mean a thing to you. You're only upset because you've been caught. What was the exact plan, anyway? How many months of blissful marriage was I going to be blessed with before you sued for divorce and a handsome settlement?"

Sloan's hair tumbled wildly over her face; her blue eyes peaked out in liquid sapphire pleading. "I wasn't —" she began with trembling lips.

For a fraction of a second it appeared as if Wesley might be softening. Then he emitted a sharp snort of disgust which effectively curtailed her words. "Spare me, Sloan. I've admitted you're a sensational actress, but you've already conned me once. Save it. I really don't want to hear any more. Ask your question."

Sloan bit through her bottom lip until it bled. All was lost. He hated her now. Her brief dream of happiness had been shattered by her own schemes, her own lies. Swallowing, she tilted her chin despite her trembling. She would hold on to her courage as he had suggested. Perhaps he could still admire her for something, even if it would sound like a futile lie to say she did love him now . . . had . . .

"Why did you go through with the wedding?" she asked quietly, her voice soft but thankfully steady. After a painful falter she added, "And why bother with yesterday?"

He shot her a glance with a shade less disdain as he continued packing, brushing by her as if she were an obstacle like a dresser or desk as he spoke.

"I'm not really sure," he admitted with a wry hint of humor. "Maybe I feel in the back of my mind that there is something I might be able to get out of this bargain myself. And, I did want you. Badly enough to marry you, since that was your price. Then yesterday . . ." He shrugged and neatly folded a stack of pressed shirts into the bag. "Yesterday, I wanted to see how thoroughly you planned to pay up while we were still going by your rules." He abruptly stopped his packing, arms crossed over his chest, and flicked his green eyes over her from head to toe with such formidable insolence that a crimson blush spread like a stain to her cheeks. "I must say, love," he spoke with the silky tone she had learned could be so cutting and dangerous, "you do pay up handsomely. I always knew, from watching the way that you moved, that you'd be dynamite in bed. Certain women are made for it. Even so, your veins must be filled with ice water for you to respond with such — talented ardor — to a man you don't love."

If he had slapped her soundly across the face, he couldn't have been more abusive. Sloan was still for a second, absorbing the shock, amazed that anyone could be so blind. Then her shock receded as anger, boiling like red-hot lava, raged through her system. She had been wrong, yes, but she didn't deserve the things he was saying.

Fear, control, and all sense of reasonable logic fell from her like a cloak, and she flew at him with the speed and wrath of a whirling tornado. "You bastard!" she hissed, and she struck him cleanly with a fury-driven open hand that left him no time to ward off the blow.

It was his turn to stand dead still as the mark she had imprinted on his face quickly turned white, pink, and dark red. The sound of her slap seemed to reverberate through the room as he slowly rubbed his cheek, staring at her all the while. "My beloved wife," he drawled mockingly, "that was certainly uncalled-for. I've been desperately trying to remain nonviolent about this whole thing."

Sloan took a deep breath of trepidation. She wisely felt the time for courage ebbing. His features, so handsome and strongly formed, were twisted into hard, grim lines; his eyes, no longer icy, blazed with a fury more intense than that of a raging sea. She began to back away, once more frightened — she didn't like his expression one bit. His eyes suddenly flickered over her again, and she realized her unprecipitated blow had dislodged her improvised sheet tunic and that he was gazing upon the mound of one creamy, exposed breast. Flushed, she pulled the sheet more tightly around her, only to be rewarded for her efforts by a dry, mirthless chuckle from Wes.

"Rather late for you to turn modest, isn't it?" he demanded scornfully. The suitcase went to the floor, and he sat on the bed. "Come here," he ordered arrogantly.

She could see the rise and fall of his black-matted chest, read the desire that burned along with the anger in his eyes. Her gaze fell to his hands, large hands, wisped with coarse strands of the same black hair, hands with fingers neatly kept, strong hands, strong fingers, capable of holding her with infinite tenderness and arousing her to abandoned passion, capable of manipulating her forcefully and bending her to his will.

Her eyes slowly left the fascination of his hands and moved upward. A single pulse beat erratically in the fine blue line of a vein in his corded neck. She raised her eyes still further, saw the ragged, crooked smile set lazily into his sensuous lips, saw that the light in his eyes held no tenderness, no love. Just hard, cold fury and desire.

She shook her head softly, beseechingly, and whispered, "No."

"Come here." The devilish grin increased as he repeated his command. His tone was

216

deceptively low and pleasant as he added, "Sloan, don't make me come to you."

Wincing, Sloan inched toward him, her eyes downcast, her thick lashes hiding the emotions that raged within them. A scuffle, she knew, would be worthless. She was probably lucky he hadn't decided to strike her back before . . . maybe, just maybe, she could talk to him. But she paused when she reached him, afraid to face him, finally lifting her lashes to meet his eyes with open pleading.

But he didn't glance into her eyes to read their message. He tugged at the sheet until it fell to the floor at her feet. The startling green gems of his eyes raked over her briefly with insolent satisfaction, then his arms came around her, and she was swept to the bed beside him. She tried to speak, but his lips claimed hers, and her words were muffled as his tongue sought her mouth with a unique mastery all its own. Then her mouth was deserted as his kisses roamed along the graceful arch of her throat and down to her breasts. But they were not gentle kisses, not even hinting at love or tenderness. They were rough and urgent; they demanded and violated. Salt tears formed in Sloan's eyes, and even as she felt a nipple harden beneath his mouth and inwardly admitted that a rousing fire was slowly coursing through her treacherous body, she protested, if somewhat breathlessly.

"Wesley — *no!*"

"No?" A single brow raised high as he lifted himself to challenge her scornfully. "And why not? You've got your ring and your money. I'm assuming this was my return offering. And, my darling," he hissed bitterly, "I haven't seen you suffering, yet."

Sloan blinked her eyes and winced, unable to move within the concrete prison of his arms. Bracing herself she began to speak. "Wesley, I will not let you make love to me like this —"

"Make love?" he interjected. "Sweet wife, it all has to be prettily wrapped and worded on the outside, huh? But you're not going to play the hypocrite anymore. You enjoy my bed, darling; to deny that would be ludicrous. And more important, dear wife, *you made the bed,* and now *you will lie in it!*"

Dismissing anything else she might have to say as inconsequential, Wesley returned casually to his sure arousal of her body. His lips were searing her flesh like hot irons, and she knew she would eventually succumb. But she had to make him listen!

"Wesley . . . wait . . . you don't understand."

"So talk to me," he murmured, his words muffled by her flesh.

"You're angry," Sloan choked, forgetting the sense she was trying to make. "You're angry," she raspily repeated herself.

His lovemaking took an abrupt halt, and he raised his head. His eyes bored into hers like hot coals, and his lips twisted savagely. "Angry!" he roared. "That has to be the understatement of the year!"

His head lowered again, and Sloan could say no more. She was swept into the storm of his savage passion, capitulated to a high of blazing ecstasy by the undeniable fervency and ardor of the chemistry that linked them. Yet as he brought her to a shuddering crescendo, tears again filled her eyes. He did not hold her to him in their mutual satisfaction. He rolled away from her, and his weight lifted from the bed. Sloan pulled the covers over her still-burning body and buried her face in the pillow.

He must have stood staring at her for several minutes because she heard his voice, soft and very close, and sensed his presence.

"Play with fire, my love, and you do get burned."

Sloan didn't turn. There had been no mockery or cruelty to his words, but the pain in her was too fresh and intense to chance another wound. He moved away, and she heard the click of the bathroom door. With him safely out of earshot, she allowed her tears of shame to run freely into her pillow. He might not know it, but she was completely his creature. Even as her mind had rebelled against his forceful demands, her betraying body had succumbed with humiliating eagerness. If only he hadn't walked in without her knowing, allowing her words to damn her. And why didn't Wesley give her a chance to explain it?

Because, she knew, it had all rung too close to the truth because it had been the truth at one time! And she had been too sure of herself, too sure that she knew all the sides there were to Wesley. But, she thought with belated remorse, she should have never made the deadly mistake of underestimating him. She had blissfully forgotten that danger could lurk in deep, quiet places.

Another click of the bathroom door informed her that Wesley was back in the room, and she dragged her head from the pillow. He was dressed, superbly handsome and cool in a baize linen jacket which emphasized the sleekness of his dark hair, the vivid green of his eyes, the bronze hue of his strongly chiseled features. He didn't bother to glance at her as he calmly hefted his suit-case to a chair and rifled his pockets for his wallet.

Sloan ran her tongue along her parched lips. "What are you doing?" she asked tone-lessly.

His eyes darted to her with a flick of amusement. "That's rather obvious, isn't it? I'm leaving you to your independent bliss."

She had to moisten her lips again. "Where are you going?"

"Paris, probably," he replied with a negligent shrug. "I need a place to cool down for a while, and I do like the city."

Why wouldn't he say something substantial? she raged silently. He had taken his revenge, why didn't he help a little now? Why was he leaving this wreck of a situation entirely up to her?

Once more she forced herself to talk. "Do you want me to go home and try for an annulment? I may have to file divorce papers. I'm not really sure how it works —"

The amusement vanished from his face to be replaced by a grim, implacable anger. "There will be no divorce . . . now," he told her, tossing a wad of bills indifferently on the bed along with a blue vinyl checkbook. "My accountant will handle your monthly bills," he continued coldly. "All you will need to worry about will be your personal expenses."

Sloan stared at it with mortified amazement. She grabbed the checkbook and bills and threw them viciously back at him before covering her face with her hands. He wasn't a wonderful man at all; he was completely insensitive, domineering, and ruthless. He had purposely made a point of tossing the money on the bed with the full intent of twisting the knife further to underline his point. Payment in full. Money for services rendered. She was nothing better to him than an overpriced call girl. Less. Women of the trade, according to him, had a certain honesty.

Her action served to rekindle his amusement. "You do have problems, my love, calling a spade a spade. You want that sugar-coating on everything. But I can't handle this thing that way. You'll remain my wife for the time being, but believe me, love, you'll stay in line. And we'll keep things honest and on the level from here on out."

Sloan had to choke back jagged, sobbing laughter. The tricks of fate were so ironic! If only Wesley hadn't overheard the *wrong half* of her conversation with Cassie. She would have admitted one day that she had originally sought him out because of desperation, but she would have explained it properly and opened her heart to tell him how she had come to love him for his quiet goodness and strength and lovingly begged his forgiveness! They could have had a life of mutual respect and adoring happiness.

It would be futile to attempt any explanations now. He would never believe her. He would probably never believe another word that came out of her mouth.

"What do you want me to do?" she asked with heartless misery, her face still buried in her hands.

"I don't know, yet," he mused. "See Brussels for the next two weeks." She sensed his offhand shrug. "When you get home, say that I was delayed on business. I'll be getting in touch with you."

Sloan finally looked up, her face tear-stained, her eyes reddened with abject despair. She was surprised to see that he still stood contemplatively in the doorway, watching her. His eyes were strangely soft for a moment, and although she knew he was feeling something for her, she didn't realize how completely she touched his heart. She was beautiful in her cocoon of sheets, her hair flared about her face in captivating disarray, her eyes wet and dazzling in their despondency. He walked back to her slowly and almost absently lifted a strand of her hair, marveling at the play of red, gold, and mahogany within its depths. A darkness filled his eyes which could have been taken for an agony as strident as Sloan's, an infinite yearning to take her in his arms and comfort and protect her.

She saw the tightening of his jaw and the moment of tenderness vanished as completely as if it had never been. Suddenly, Sloan couldn't take any more; she lashed out at him as coldly as he had her.

"I thought you were leaving."

His body stiffened perceptively, and she felt a mute satisfaction at wounding him after the terrible thrusts he had delivered to her. "Oh, I am going," Wesley said grimly. "This isn't exactly what I had in mind for a honeymoon either. Watch your step carefully, Sloan. I will be back."

"Why?" she demanded, rising haughtily to his threat. "You've made it rather clear what you think of me."

"True," Wesley countered sardonically. "But then, what difference does that make? You were willing to marry me while not loving me, why should it matter if I'm no longer enamored of you?"

"I never hated you," Sloan said bleakly.

Wes was still for a minute, then his finger

hooked her chin to bring her face up to meet his. "I don't hate you," he said quietly. "In all honesty, I don't know what I feel. A lot of anger and humiliation at the moment, and that's why I'm leaving."

"Then go!" Sloan rasped icily. She wanted the words back as soon as they left her mouth, but once spoken, they couldn't be retrieved. He had spoken to her kindly; he had given her a golden opportunity to leave a salvageable thread in their marriage. But her own pain and confusion had registered only that he was leaving, walking out on her after showering her with verbal abuse and proving his physical mastery.

Words began to tumble from her mouth in a spew of unmeant venom. "I'm not so sure about you, Mr. Adams, either. You're not the man I thought you. You haven't a shred of compassion in your entire being, and you're about as kindly as a great white shark. You're ruthless, cruel, and vicious. Definitely not nice."

"That's enough!" Wes stated with frigid finality. The muscles were working in his jaw, and as Sloan stared up at him, she knew he was fighting a fierce battle for self-control. To his credit, he won.

"I never saw myself as walking benevolence," he told her, catching the sides of her hair and gripping them tautly to hold her face to his, "but then I do tend to be a fairly tolerant soul. You have to admit, Sloan, that the provocation has been great. I probably am a nice man, darling, I'm just not the complete puppet you took me to be." His pull on her hair tightened for just a second and then released. He gazed at her for a moment longer, his mouth a grim, white line, and then turned for his suitcase and the door.

"Oh," he added, pausing with his hand on the knob. "Do us both a favor and remember one thing. You are married. Should you forget it, darling, after all the rest, I might be severely tempted to follow my first inclination and break that lovely little neck. And I will be back, hopefully civil by the time I reach Gettysburg." He raised his brows in a high arch of mocking speculation. "You do get my drift?"

Blue and green eyes locked in a cold stare. "I get your drift," she retorted defiantly.

"Good. It's one thing to be taken for a fool, love, but I promise I won't wear horns as well." His teeth ground together, and his tone became pained. "I don't ever want to subject myself to a repeat of today's performance." Then the pain and bitterness were harshly grated over; they might have been imagined. "I usually do discover things — as belated as it may be."

His eyes slid over her slowly in a last assessment; he didn't seem to expect any more answers — and she had none to give him. His gaze came back to hers in a final challenge.

Sloan's gaze fell from Wesley's, and sadly, she missed the gamut of torn emotions that raced through his eyes. In her stunned state of agonized confusion, it was doubtful she would have recognized them anyway.

Because he was split into more pieces than she.

As he stared at her, he was struck again with awe at her beauty. The sapphire eyes; the wild tangle of hair that held more colors than a rainbow — hair that could entangle a man and spin him helplessly into a drowning lair forever; the exquisite, supple body that was wiry, sweetly curved, unceasingly graceful . . . A dancer's form; an angel's face.

He had been in love with her his entire adult life — adulating her from afar, never finding peace or satisfaction because he knew she existed in the world and he was not close to her.

And then it had seemed that she was his.

He was a strong man; he had taken on life and received fame and fortune. In return, he had paid his dues with decency and fairness. Knowing his own power, he had never willingly hurt another person. But he had never felt anything like the gut-wrenching pain of betrayal; the gnawing agony that seemed to eat away at his insides, bit by excruciating bit.

Betrayal by the woman he idolized over his own life.

And he had lashed out with full intent to wound. Not physically; he could snap her in half and he knew it, but because of his size, he had long since learned to control the forces of rage. No, he had gone after her with the strongest weapon known to man, words, calculated to rip and shred. . . .

But he had lost control of the words — gone further than he ever meant. He winced now at his own cruelty, but none of it could be undone. . . .

He had to come to terms with himself. She had used him and made a complete fool of him. But he still loved her, and the pain he had caused her was hurting him. Yet he couldn't go to her now — he couldn't erase any of what had happened.

And he couldn't forget that she had purposely seduced him into marriage for money.

But he couldn't give her up. Somewhere

in the future. . . .

Which was not now. His pride, ego, and heart were all wounded, raw and bleeding. If he stayed, her very beauty and his love for her would heighten his pain, and he would say more words that couldn't be taken back . . . that could never be forgiven.

She looked at him again, her crystal blue eyes brimming, but defiant, and hateful. As if a shutter had fallen over them, his own eyes gave nothing more away. "Good-bye, Sloan," he said softly.

And the door slammed coldly in her face.

She didn't cry again; she was numb with disbelief. For at least an hour she didn't even move, but remained lifelessly in the bed, staring straight ahead at the tapestried wall, unable to think and sort her whirling emotions. Then she finally obeyed the little voice that told her she had to do something, rose mechanically, and situated herself in the shower. Her hands began to steady as the hot water waved over them, and she finally forced herself to accept the situation.

A part of her hated Wesley for the things he had said and done, for taking her and using her so brutally simply to prove that he knew her game and was changing the rules. She had sold out, and in his vengeance, he wanted her to know that she was now his and that when he said jump, her question should be, How high?

And a part of her hated herself. Color that was more than the force of the hot water filled her skin at the thought of her uninhibited response to him despite everything. Granted, the release of the anger Wesley had been harboring had created the passionate desire of the morning, and he would have taken her roughly in that bed no matter what her reaction. But Lord! she thought sickly, he had manhandled her, thrown her around, called her everything just short of tramp — albeit with a modicum of control — and she had protested but feebly and clung to him in wanton pleasure with gutteral whimperings in her throat that proved her to be an easily assailable toy. . . .

"Damn, I hate him!" she raged aloud to the cascading water. But she didn't. She still loved him, desperately, and a part of her even understood the violence of his reaction. He had loved her, really loved her, and as far as he could see, she had laughingly tossed that love aside.

There was still hope, she told herself, turning off the water. He had said he would come back. And when he did, his initial rage would be gone. She would talk to him. . . .

Her hands flew back to her face, and she

shuddered. How could she talk to him if he continued to treat her as he did today? Her own temper would flare, and they would enter one disastrous argument after another.

No! she decided firmly. There would be no more repeats of today. Wesley was not a primitive caveman wielding a club, nor was she a helpless female at his mercy. Whether he ever decided to believe her or trust in her or not, they couldn't have any relationship without a semblance of dignity. She loved him, but she couldn't bear for this to go on . . . him nonchalantly pulling her about as if she were a puppet, there for his amusement and then cast aside at his whimsy.

Maybe it was best he didn't know how completely and thoroughly she loved him. He could wedge his knives so much more deeply. Perhaps he should go on thinking her a cold, heartless schemer.

She was still trembling, shaking like a leaf blown high in winter. I've got to pull myself together! she wailed silently. But her dreams, so good, so wonderful . . . love, comfort . . . the security of being loved and cared for . . . had just been cruelly shattered in that same winter wind. She couldn't pull herself together; she couldn't even get out of the shower.

Sloan eventually did get out of the shower. She dressed; she even picked up the guide books Wes had left behind. A picture of Waterloo loomed before her . . . statues of Lord Nelson and Napoleon. Bruges . . . ancient walled city. Ostend.

Places and things they should have seen together. . . .

Sloan brushed the brochures to the floor. Tears flooded her eyes. She couldn't stay in Belgium . . . one brochure caught her attention. It was for the ferry that left the coast of Normandy for the fabled White Cliffs of Dover.

She would go to England, she decided dully.

But it was three days before she could even leave the room.

# CHAPTER NINE

By the time Sloan returned to Gettysburg she had done a fair job of pulling herself together — or at least an acceptable job of creating a smooth shell to hide behind and a serene mask with which to face the world.

The mask was brittle, and beneath it she was a desolate and miserable wreck, but no one would ever know. To complicate matters, she had no idea what Wesley's next move might be, but since he had adamantly decreed that there would be no divorce, she was nervously determined to keep up appearances on the slender line of hope that something could be worked out.

She hadn't stayed in Belgium. After finally managing to emerge from her room, she found the memories of Brussels too haunting and beautifully ironic to bear. Besides, though of French descent, she had none of Wesley's gift for the language, and Flemish eluded her completely. She had moved across the English channel to Dover

233

and on to London where she had forced herself to sightsee like crazy. For hours she had gazed upon the ancient tombs and history of Westminster Abbey, toured the endless halls of the Victoria and Albert, and strolled the shops of Piccadilly Circus and Carnaby Street. Her greatest pleasure, however, had been a day spent in the London Dungeon — a wax museum specializing in the rather barbaric practices of the various tribes and nationalities that combined to make the English people. With a spite she wasn't quite able to contain, she thought how nice it would be to contain Wes in a gibbet, boil him in oil, or set him to the rack. Her pleasure didn't last, however, because she knew she had no desire for real vengeance, only a yearning to go back in time and undo all the wrong between them and recapture the wonderfully golden moments when they had both been truly in love.

Nothing could be undone. She had to brace herself for the dubious future, steady frayed nerves that threatened to snap with the pressure of wondering when she would suddenly look up and discover Wes had returned.

With just the right amount of dejection Sloan informed Florence that Wes had been held up on business. She breathed a little more easily when Florence accepted her explanation without doubt — apparently Wes traveled frequently on business.

She didn't need to feign her happiness at her reunion with her children, nor stifle the delight that the children's pleasure over their foreign gifts gave her.

It was hardest to see Cassie. She didn't dare give away the slightest trauma — if Cassie were to discover that her trip of concern to her sister's house had been the catalyst to the destruction of her marriage, she would never forgive herself. Still, it was very, very difficult to listen to Cassie's sympathy for "poor Wes," working two weeks after his wedding away from his bride. . . .

Sloan was extremely grateful for her own work, and she plunged her heart and soul into her classes. But as the weeks began to pass and no word was heard from Wes, her resolve to remain cool and collected despite the inner battle played beneath her shell became increasingly arduous. She kept up a strained smile when asked about Wes, always sighing and saying that he had called and was regrettably still delayed.

Finals for the students came and went, sending Sloan into mental chaos. She would have plenty of time to spend with the kids, but Florence had the house in complete control, and since the children loved their summer day school, she would have hours of nothing to do but chew her nails and worry and give vent to the tears that always lurked behind her eyes when no one was looking.

She was looking at the mess that was her attempted cleanup of her desk on the last day of classes, when an idea that had been vaguely forming at the back of her head rose to the surface with vehemence. Leaving papers and folders to flutter in her wake, she raced into Jim's office.

"Jim!" she exclaimed, interrupting his study of a thesis.

"Sloan!" he imitated her urgent tone with a chuckle. "What is it?"

Curling into the chair that faced his desk — an identical arrangement to her own office — she plunged right in before she could lose her nerve and determined impetus. "Have you thought any more about setting up your own school?"

Jim sighed and shrugged. "I've thought about it, but that's about all. I'm not really in shape yet to try my own wings."

"But I am!" Sloan whispered softly.

"What?"

"Think about it!" Sloan urged excitedly, planting her elbows on the desk as her

236

dream took flight. "I can swing the financial end, you can handle administrative problems, and we both teach and eventually form a first-rate company. What do you think?"

"Sloan" — Jim shook his head — "you're not even going to be here —"

"Oh, I have a feeling it will be a long, long time before we make the actual move to Kentucky," she said dryly, wondering herself if she would ever be asked to accompany her husband to his home. "And besides," she added hastily, expecting his further objections, "it will be a business, a partnership. If I do leave, you hire another teacher, and since I know it would be a success, the investment would still be worthwhile."

Jim scratched his forehead thoughtfully, hesitating with his reply, but Sloan could see the light of anticipation dawning in his eyes. "Have you discussed this with Wes?" he asked.

"No," Sloan answered slowly. Then she bit down hard onto her jaw, remembering the taunting way he had tossed the money and cards on the bed in Belgium — payment for services rendered. "I'm sure Wes isn't going to care," she said, biting back the taste of bitterness the words cost her. "We'll be returning it all eventually."

"Sloan," Jim advised uncertainly, "you're talking I don't know how many thousands —"

"Don't worry about the money," she interrupted quickly. "I'll handle that end of it." She scribbled the names and addresses of Wesley's attorney and accountant on a scratch pad and pushed it toward him. "Just be in the lawyer's office a week from Monday."

From that point on, Sloan gave little heed to the repercussions that might fall her way if Wes did return before she was set. He had been gone over a month without a single word, and though her heart often ached with a physical pain, she was hardening. Her ambition to set up her own school and dance company had her captured in a whirlpool she was powerless to stop or deny, and the whirlpool was swirling away with no hindrance.

Florence thought the idea wonderful; so did Wesley's attorney and his accountant — the latter telling Sloan that if all did fall apart, Wes could take a healthy tax break. She wasn't particularly fond of his lack of faith, but she didn't really care as long as he was helping her.

And thankfully, Wes had informed no one

that he wasn't on the best of terms with his wife. She had feared at first that he might have put restrictions on her expenditures, but that was obviously not the case. The accountant didn't blink an eye when she held her breath and rattled off the sums she would need.

On the first day of fall her school was opened. As she and Jim had hoped, they were besieged by past and present students of the college who wanted to engage in more serious study.

"This is going to be a success," Jim said with awe as he looked over their records at the end of the day.

"Of course!" Sloan laughed teasingly. "We have to be the best this side of Philadelphia!"

"I hope so," Jim said fervently, "I just wish —"

Sloan cut him off, knowing his reference would be to Wes. She had become so accustomed to inventing phone calls and conversations with her husband that she didn't even think as the next reassuring lie slipped from her lips. "Oh, didn't I tell you? I talked to Wes last night, and he thinks the whole thing is marvelous! He still doesn't know when he'll be back, and this will keep me busy and off the streets."

★ ★ ★

She was kept busy. Another two weeks saw their venture in full swing. Although the work load didn't keep Sloan's mind from wondering achingly about her husband, it did keep her on an even keel. The studio was beautiful — she had grown increasingly ostentatious as she discovered the flow of her seemingly unlimited funds, and they offered every amenity to their classes. A smile that wasn't entirely happy but purely satisfied was on her lips when Jim ambled into their mutual, roomy, shag-rugged and leather-furnished office after his last tap class at five.

"Patty Smith is waiting for you down in the studio," he advised her with a tired but pleased grin. "I'll finish up in here while you get started with her. Then I'll be back down, and we can lock up together." He frowned slightly. "What's Patty doing here now anyway?"

"Private lesson," Sloan said with a wry smile. "She has an audition for the Solid Gold dancers on Monday, and we're going to work on the number she'll be doing — sprucing up at the last minute."

"Oh," Jim nodded sagely. "Hey," he asked as they both walked to the connecting door, "heard from Wes? Think he'll be impressed with the place?"

"Oh — ah, yes and yes," Sloan mumbled as she walked past him. "I, uh, talked to him last night, and he's still detained, but I'm sure he'll be quite surprised by our success." She lowered her head and winced as she hurried to the studio. Wes sure as hell was going to be surprised — if he ever returned. She was beginning to think the entire thing had been a fabulous dream that had turned to a painful nightmare at the end. But it wasn't a dream; the gold band and diamond cluster on her finger weighed heavily to remind her of reality.

Patty was a good dancer. Her instinctive grasp of dance was a natural talent, and Sloan had hopes that her student would succeed with her audition. She lost track of thought and time as she tutored her pupil. It was a fast, rugged piece, performed to a number by a popular rock group, indicative of the work she would be doing if she got her job.

"It's good, Patty, really good," Sloan told the anxious girl. "Just watch your timing. Let the music be your guide." She sighed as Patty stared at her blankly. "I'll run it through, Patty. Listen to the music while you watch."

Sloan set the stereo and moved into

Patty's dance, allowing the beat of the music to permeate her limbs and guide her. Her concentration was entirely on the harmonious tempo of movement; she was heedless of anything around her. As the song neared its end, she rose in a high leap, one leg kicked before her, the other arched at her back, her toe touching her head.

It was then that she saw Wes, leaning nonchalantly in the doorway, his dark suit impeccably cut, hands in his pockets, his eyes glittering with a hard jade gleam as he watched her, that crooked smile that wasn't a smile at all set pleasantly into his features as he listened casually to whatever it was that an enthusiastic Jim was saying to him.

Sloan almost fell. She had a streaking vision of herself crumpled on the floor, her limbs twisted and broken.

But she didn't fall. She landed supplely and finished the piece for Patty, her thoughts whirling at a speed more intense than the rock music. She should have been prepared, but she wasn't. She was in shock.

Her eyes clenched tightly as she struggled to hold back tears of uncertainty. Had he finally come to call it quits? To tell her he had extracted whatever revenge he had required and that their best course now was a divorce?

Her heart was pounding tumultuously, and she knew it was more than the dance. She had learned painfully to live without Wes, but seeing him cut open every wound. He seemed to exude that overpowering masculinity which had first entrapped her senses as he stood there, so tall, so broad and yet achingly trim, the lines of his physique emphasized by the tailored cut of his suit. The profile, though hard, was still the one she had fallen in love with. . . . Her eyes flicked from the full sensual lips that could claim hers with such mastery to the hands that dealt pleasure even as they mocked. . . .

If only his eyes weren't so cold and hard . . . relentless, ruthless, and condemning now, contemptuous when they lit upon her.

She was shaking as the music ended, and she struggled for control. She loved him, and she wanted their marriage to work no matter how the odds appeared to be irrevocably against them. Now was her chance to at least show that she was willing. . . .

"Patty, keep working," she told the girl hastily, rushing to the doorway. She forced herself to be calm even as she longed to throw herself into his arms, even as her eyes glimmered brilliantly with hope.

She stopped a foot away from Wes, halted by the chill in his eyes. She had no chance to take the initiative — he had already taken it and thankfully quelled her desire to throw herself at him before she made a fool of herself.

"Darling," he said coolly, brushing frigid lips against her forehead and encircling a cold arm of steel lightly around her waist. "Jim was just thanking me for sanctioning this little venture."

Sloan stiffened miserably within his grasp, knowing how he mocked her. She met his gaze with crystal defiance, miserably praying he wouldn't defrock her series of lies before Jim and that she wouldn't hit the end of her nerves and burst into the tears she was sure he would love. And still he had her hypnotized, trembling beneath her barrier of ice, wishing so desperately that she could forget everything and curl into his arms, satiate herself with the male power and light dizzying scent that radiated from him....

"We are a success, as you can see," she said quickly, forcing a stiff smile. "Your investment will be made back in our first year."

"Will it?" Wes inquired politely.

"Yes, I really believe it will!" Jim said with innocent enthusiasm. He laughed as he realized neither Sloan nor Wes really paid attention to him. "This must be some surprise for you both. Sloan said you didn't think you'd be in for some time when you spoke to her last night!"

"Did you say that, darling?" Wes asked Sloan, his dagger gaze turning fully to her and his lips curling sardonically.

Sloan moistened her lips, hating him at that moment, ready to scream if he didn't clear things one way or another.

"Yes, I decided to surprise her," Wes continued in his pleasant tone with the iron edge. "And I certainly am surprised myself, darling. I never expected such professionalism when we, uh, *discussed,* your business." He brushed a damp strand of hair from Sloan's face. "That was quite a dance you were doing when I walked in, Sloan. 'Cold As Ice,' wasn't that the tune?" he inquired politely, his sardonic smile still nicely in place. He had missed his wife's expression of pleading when she saw him; she had carried off her reserve and dignity so well as she approached him that he had no idea that she was longing to see him, praying for his loving touch. All he saw was the woman who had admittedly married him for his money, who now appeared to be annoyed that he had come home to watch her spend it . . . the woman he had loved half his life . . . still loved. . . . "Cold As Ice," he repeated pleasantly, nor waiting for her reply and murmuring his last comment as if he teased someone. "What is it, sweetheart, your theme song?"

Sloan grinned along with Jim's unknowing laughter, but she felt a shivering chill streak along her back. She knew he wasn't teasing, and she dreaded the confrontation coming between them when they were alone. She vowed as she forced that grin that she would never break to him; if he had pegged her as cold and mercenary and now despised her still, she would never let him know how the tables had turned and she pined for his love. "Yes," she teased as he had, but her eyes glared like blue ice into his, "my theme song."

"Lord," Jim jumped in, absurdly unaware of the tension that filled the air around them. "Here I am interrupting you two when you've already had a honeymoon interrupted. Sloan, Wes — go home, or wherever you two newlyweds want to be after a separation. I'll finish up with Patty and lock up."

"No," Sloan started so protest, fear of being with her husband alone suddenly gripping her fiercely. But Wesley overrode her protest.

"Thanks, Jim," he said, straightening and running a cold, taunting finger along Sloan's cheek, making her bite her lip to keep from flinching. "I would like to be alone with my, uh, wife." He dropped his hand from her face. "Get your things, Sloan." It was softly spoken, but undeniably a command.

Rigid with anger and the fear she couldn't quite squelch, Sloan lowered her eyes and opted for obedience. She had to face him sooner or later.

"I have my own car —" she started briskly as they left the school and Jim behind, "Cold As Ice" once more blaring from the stereo.

"Leave it," Wes said just as briskly. "We can get it tomorrow."

Sloan shrugged and walked along with him to the Lincoln, poker-faced as he opened her door and ushered her in. She was sure he was going to rail into her immediately, tearing her apart piece by piece for her actions during his absence. He was strangely silent instead, his attention on his driving, his hardened jaw and cold eyes rigid in the profile she glanced at covertly from the lowered shade of her lashes. It seemed to Sloan that the tension in the car mounted until it was thick and tangible and

247

she was drowning in it. "Don't you think we should talk," she finally exploded, unable to bear the uncertainty a moment longer. "I really don't care to argue in front of the children," she added with cold hauteur.

His eyes slid from the road to her for a moment, searing her with disdainful ice. His hand shot across the car, and she flinched thinking he was coming for her, but he wasn't. He snapped the button on the glove compartment and the door fell open. With his eyes back on the road, he felt for a plump envelope, found it, tossed it on her lap, and slammed the door closed.

"I have no intention of arguing in front of the children," he said, "but neither am I in a mood to discuss anything with you while driving. Don't worry, the children are not at the house."

"What?" Sloan exclaimed, baffled by his words and the envelope lying in her lap. She glanced from it to Wes, afraid to touch it, unaware of what it might contain. "Where are the children?" she demanded.

"At a motel by Hershey Park by now, I would imagine," Wes replied briefly.

The import of his words sank slowly into Sloan's mind, and she was then struck by a fury that overwhelmed her in shattering waves. *"What?"* she shrieked, twisting to face him in the car. "How dare you send my children away, how dare you take it upon yourself —"

"They aren't your children anymore, Sloan; check the envelope on your lap. It's the final judgment. Legally, they are my children now, too." His gaze flicked to her steaming face with a quelling authority. "I didn't send them away, I sent them on a little vacation — with Cassie and George as well as Florence."

"A little vacation!" Sloan repeated incredulously, pushing the envelope from her lap to the floor with vengeance as she struggled against tears of anger and the impulse to fling herself at him and cause any bodily harm that she could. "You bastard!" she hissed. "You decide to waltz back in and just flick them aside —"

"You can stop now, Sloan!" Wesley's voice growled low with the sharp edge of deadly warning. "I'm not flicking anyone aside; I'm more aware of their welfare at the moment than you are. You want to hide behind them. I think it's going to be to their benefit not to be around while you and I settle the immediate future."

"I don't see where there is a future. Immediate or otherwise," Sloan hissed, grudgingly admitting to herself that the concern he was showing the children was sincere, but she wasn't about to say so. She was still seething with a rage that was in part a debilitating jealousy that she abhorred. Where had he been for all this time? . . . "Since you haven't bothered with a call for six weeks," she said aloud, "I hardly see any justice to your sweeping in like the north wind and thinking you can call the shots —"

"I will call the shots," he interrupted her curtly, "and that should be no surprise to you; I told you as much in Belgium. And if we're discussing justice, Mrs. Adams, let's bear in mind that you owe me."

"I don't owe you anything!" Sloan snapped. "You've already subjected me to payment in full."

Wes laughed, startling her with an honest twinge of amusement. "Payment in full? Taking a look at that school I so magnanimously funded makes you more in debt than ever."

Sloan crunched down on her lip uncomfortably. "You'll get your money back," she said with quiet conviction.

"I believe I will," Wes said indifferently. He raised a brow in her direction. "I don't remember ever accusing you of stupidity."

The car pulled into the house drive before Sloan could think of a reply to his double-edged statement. Sloan hopped out before he could come around and assist her and hurried for the front door, fumbling in her bag for her key. To her dismay it eluded her fingers and Wes was twisting the lock while she still fumbled. "Allow me," he mocked her, pushing open the door and ushering her in.

The house seemed empty and hostile with Florence and the children gone, fueling Sloan's fury that Wes should send the kids off without her approval. Deciding to ignore his dominating presence until she could rally from the shock of his sudden arrival, she dropped her things and stalked for the shower. Apparently, he didn't mind if the night was spent in slow torture. She might as well shower and be comfortable while she regathered her forces.

"What's for dinner?" he called after her, as if they returned home together every night of the week.

"How should I know?" Sloan shot back. "You're the one who sent the housekeeper away."

She was careful to bolt the shower door, but he made no attempt to come near. Emerging a half hour later with her skin pruned and her mind no closer to an answer on how to handle the impending evening, she found Wesley's travel things had all been neatly put away in her room. A rush of heated blood suffused her, but she wouldn't allow herself to remember the exotic pleasure of his arms. She'd be damned before she slept with a man who continued to treat her as Wes did. Belting a quilted housecoat securely around her waist, she took several deep breaths and headed out to meet her tiger.

Stripped of jacket and tie, the neck of his shirt open and his sleeves rolled up, Wes was reading the paper, annoyingly at home with his long lap stretched out on the coffee table, his socked feet crossed. He didn't look up as she entered the room, and for a moment she thought he didn't realize that she was there. But than he spoke, his eyes still on the paper.

"I repeat, what's for dinner?"

"And I repeat," Sloan paled with hostility, "how should I know?"

The paper landed on the coffee table with a whack, and Wes was on his feet. "Then let's find out together, shall we?" He wasn't really expecting an answer; his hand lit upon her elbow with determination and he propelled rather than escorted her into the kitchen.

Sloan spun ahead of him, tears burning

behind her eyelids. She wasn't going to stand any more of the uncertainty, of the terrible fear that he was playing cat and mouse before pouncing with his demand for a divorce. Choking, she whirled on him, determined to have it out.

"Just get it over with, Wes!" she blurted angrily.

He stared at her with drawn brows and genuine confusion. "Get what over with?" he demanded impatiently.

"Tell me how you want to arrange the divorce, and then we can stop all this and you can go somewhere for dinner!" Sloan said quickly so as not to allow her voice to tremble.

He watched her for a moment and then turned to the refrigerator to rummage through it. "I don't want a divorce," he said blandly. "I want something to eat; I'm starving."

Relief made her shake all over again, but it was a nervous relief. She had no idea of where he had been for all that time, and he had yet to give her the slightest sign that he had decided he still cared for her in the least.

"Are you sure?" she asked.

Sloan instantly became convinced that he didn't really give a damn one way or another. His reply was not a joke; it was issued with exasperation.

"Of course I'm sure. I came in this morning and I haven't eaten since."

Gritting her teeth, her voice tight, Sloan asked again, "I mean, are you sure you don't want a divorce?"

"Dammit," he muttered, slamming the refrigerator door. "You spend money like water and there's nothing to eat in this house!" His eyes turned to her, the jade speculative and hooded. "At the moment, Mrs. Adams, I do not want a divorce." His gaze followed her form, and then he walked to the telephone, dialing as he added, *"I've decided there's something I just may be able to get out of this signed and sealed bargain of yours."*

Sloan felt as if she had been hit, sure his "bargain" referred to her. She willed away the wash of humiliation that assailed her and clenched down on her teeth. She knew Wes's temper; if she had expected mercy, she had been a fool. Still, she loved him, and she wanted her marriage to work and he wasn't demanding a divorce. She didn't intend to accept his dominating scorn, but she could make an effort at a little civility by swallowing her pride for the moment and attempting to put them on a level where they could converse rationally. If they could only build up a friendship. . . .

"Who are you calling?" she asked huskily.

"Information," he replied. "Give me the name of any restaurant that delivers."

"Don't bother," she said, adding hastily at his frown, "I'm sure I can make omelettes or something."

Wes hung up the phone. "That would be fine," he said. "I think I did see a carton of eggs."

Walking around the kitchen as she prepared their meal, Sloan began to regret her offer. She could feel Wesley's keen jade gaze on her with every step and movement she made. Panic began to assail her in mammoth proportions. He said he didn't want a divorce — at the moment. But what good was having the legal contract that bound him to her — the contract she had strived so hard to achieve! — when nothing was right between them and she was constantly on tenterhooks wondering when his scorpion's sting would strike next? The cold ferocity of the anger he had shown her in Belgium had somewhat dissipated, but his comments tonight proved he didn't intend to forgive and forget. Was it because he still didn't believe she loved him, or had he lost all love and respect for her?

"You could be useful," she muttered irritably, thinking that if he stared at her any longer she would throw the entire carton of eggs into the air and fly into a laughing tantrum as they fell. "I'd like a drink."

"Scotch?" he inquired politely

"Please."

It was almost worse having him pad silently around her on his stocking feet. She was going to add that she'd like a double, but the portion he poured her while looking ironically into her eyes displayed his ability to read her like a book. "Thanks," she murmured, accepting the rock glass he offered her.

Cheese, ham, and peppers went into her omelettes. Wes continued to watch her, leaning over the counter, drinking his bourbon. She was feeling the terrible urge to do something erratic again — anything — to break the comfortable tension between them when Wes finally spoke.

"Sloan."

She glanced at him warily, but his expression was unreadable.

"I'm sorry."

Her eyes fell quickly back to the eggs browning in the pan, tears stinging her lids again. Sorry about what? she wondered. His dry remarks tonight, the fiasco of a honeymoon, or the wedding itself?

"Would you like to say something, please?" he questioned, a tinge of annoyance seeping into his tone. "I said I'm sorry."

"About what?" Sloan forced herself to ask aloud.

"Belgium."

She remained silent, desolately thinking that things had changed much since then. Jealousy — the nightmares of him with a multitude of faceless women that had gnawed away at her during his absence — and the painful memory of his hard glare when they had met again kept her from accepting his words and perhaps setting things straight when her impulse was to fly to him and tell him how terribly sorry she was too. Her hand froze on the spatula as she began to realize her impulse might be the one thing to give her a chance at her marriage. But then the moment was gone.

"Dammit! Sloan! Say something," Wes grated.

"What do you want me to say?" she charged in retaliation. "That it's all right? It isn't! You were terrible, and you haven't improved an iota."

She heard the sharp clink of his glass hitting the counter, but other than that, he controlled his temper. "I see," he said smoothly. "I was terrible — my actions were unforgivable. But it's okay that Sloan decided she could live just fine with a man she could lead by a little rope just so long as that man was filthy rich."

"Go to hell," Sloan hissed, dropping the spatula on the eggs. "Prima's Pizza delivers, or you can finish this yourself. I'm going to bed."

"Oh, no, no, no, you're not, Mrs. Adams," Wes said grimly, his hand clamping on her wrist as she attempted to walk past him. "We have a lot to talk about tonight, and we haven't even begun to scratch the surface." He released her wrist and stalked to the stove to scoop the omelettes from the pan to a plate. Inclining his head toward the kitchen table, he added, "Sit, please."

"May I fix myself another drink first?" Sloan asked with mock subservience, her eyes wide in sarcasm.

"Drink all you like, Sloan, but please do sit."

She poured herself another drink, stared at the glass, and heaped another portion of scotch into it. Maybe she could blur the razor edges of what was to come. . . .

"Do *you* want a divorce, Sloan?" Wesley plopped the food on the table and pulled out a chair for her as he asked the question.

She lowered her eyes as she slid into the chair, her fingers tightly gripped around the glass. She was caught off guard, expecting a further battle not an almost indifferent query.

"Do you?" He sat down himself, and again she knew he stared at her, his seering jade gaze giving nothing but bluntly allowing her no quarter.

"No," she finally managed to whisper.

"Why not?" he demanded.

God, why was he doing this to her, she wondered. "What do you mean?"

"I mean, why do you want to stay married? Is the money worth living with a monster you can't forgive?"

Now was the time, she knew, to say something, to drop her pride . . . but she was so afraid he was setting her up. . . . "Yes," she said coolly. "I could say that I love you, but since you're not going to believe it, let's just leave it at cold cash. A signed and sealed bargain, as you say," Her voice suddenly cracked and broke. He had tried to apologize, and she had made a mess of it. "I'm sorry, Wes," she continued with a waver. "I do want to stay married, but God, not like this! Not like Belgium! Not with you gone for weeks at a time when I have no idea where you are or who you're. . . ." She stopped speaking and took a sip of the scotch she had stared at while she spoke.

"Did you care where I was?" Wes asked softly.

"Yes," she admitted to the amber liquid swimming before her.

"Did you really care, Sloan?" he persisted. "Or was your ego bruised? Never mind," he answered himself, adding with a trace of bitterness. "I wouldn't know whether to believe you or not."

He fell silent and Sloan chewed on her lower lip. "Wes?" she finally said quietly.

"Yes?"

"Could we try to be friends?" she asked tentatively.

His arm stretched across the table, he gripped her chin, firmly but gently, forcing her to look at him. "I didn't come back to argue with you, Sloan," he said gravely, and for the first time that night she sensed a thread of an emotion that hinted of tenderness in his eyes. "It doesn't change things, but I am very sorry for my behavior in Belgium. I can't promise I'm going to be a saint from here on out; I have an ego myself and believe me, it's very bruised. You have to expect a few snide remarks when you marry a man for his money, but yes, although I find it ironic to be discussing friendship with my wife, I should hope that we work toward that end since we both plan to keep the . . . bargain . . . going."

His touch upon her chin was wearing through the thin veneer that was left on her nerves. The callused gentleness of his hand brought back sweeping memories that combined with the nearness of him — the light but fully masculine scent that would forever be imbedded in her mind, the breadth of shoulder that was so enticing to lean against, the cleanly chiseled lines of his powerful profile — to nearly engulf her senses and bring her flying to him, promising anything, pleading, begging, anything to be back in his arms, held tenderly even if it was a mockery of love.

She couldn't allow herself to do that. They had to establish a wave of communication and respect first.

She stood, praying her blurring eyes and quivering voice would not betray her need. "Tomorrow," she said tentatively, "I'd like to tell you about the school."

"Fine," he replied.

"You don't mind about it, do you?" she said hesitantly.

"No, I don't. But I will be interested in seeing your books — I don't care what you spent, but perhaps I can be helpful on the business end."

"Thank you," Sloan murmured. She needed to get away from him, and he hadn't protested her rising. "I, umm, I think I pushed it a little with the scotch. I'm going to bed. I see that your things are in my room, so I'll just move out to the —"

"No, you *won't!*" Wes interrupted sharply, the cold, guarded glimmer slipping back over his eyes as he stared at her with full attention.

"Wes," Sloan said slowly, "I'm not talking about any permanent situation —"

"Forget it," he said curtly. "Permanent, temporary, or otherwise. In my book, a husband and wife share a room."

She was too tired and too frazzled to realize what she said next. "Terry would have —" Her voice broke off with abrupt dismay.

Wes stood. It seemed as if he did it very slowly, rising over her with a towering force that was chilling although they were several feet apart. His fingers were clenched tightly around a napkin, the knuckles white, the thin line of his grimly twisted lips just as devoid of color.

"I think we discussed this once," he said with soft danger. "I am not Terry. I do not sleep on couches, nor will you. *I am not Terry.*"

Sloan met his gaze, dismayed at the hard-core jade. He still intended to tell her just how high to jump. . . .

"No," she agreed scathingly. "You are not Terry. Terry was a nice man." She spun on him before he could retaliate and sought refuge in her bedroom, staring long at the lock on the door. She pushed it in, but then released it as his voice tauntingly followed her.

"Don't bother, Sloan. If you're in my — our — room, a lock isn't going to stop me from entering."

He didn't come to bed for a long, long time. Sloan lay in silent misery, her nerves and, yes, anticipation fighting sleep. Each time she heard a movement in the house, she jumped while her mind raced double-time. Damn! She did want him so badly, being near him and not touching him was like slow and torturous starvation. . . .

But all she really had now was a piece of paper and her pride. She couldn't allow herself to show how vulnerable she was. . . .

He entered the room in the dark, and she barely breathed, feigning deep sleep, hearing the sounds as he undressed as if each piece of clothing had fallen with the burst of an explosion. He crawled in beside her, and her entire body went stiff, her heart seemed to thunder, and her flesh was painfully aware of his heat as she waited. . . .

And waited.

He didn't touch her. He plumped his pillow, adjusted his position, stretched his body out comfortably. But didn't touch her.

Sloan lay in shocked confusion. And, she realized sinkingly, disappointment. Whatever she had been telling herself was a lie. She had been glad that he had insisted upon sleeping together; she had been wonderfully relieved that he was going to force her into his arms so that she would have an excuse to salve her pride.

But now she just ached, her disappointment becoming a physical agony.

She didn't know how long she lay there, her eyes open, staring blankly into the dark, when he shifted again, and his arm grazed her shoulder.

"What is the matter with you?" Wes demanded impatiently, obviously aware she had never been sleeping. "You're as cold and stiff as marble and shivering like a rabbit."

"I — I —" Sloan stammered.

She heard his soft chuckle; it was a gentle

sound of amusement, and it caressed her warmth. "I see," he said, and although his voice was amused, it was tender. "You thought I was going to force you into keeping conjugal rights. No, my love, I'll not force you. I won't sleep in another room, but I won't force you."

"You . . . you don't want to make love?" Sloan said in a strangled voice.

She felt his hand on her cheek, the knuckles grazing her flesh, his whisper soft and gentle. "I didn't say that. But I want you to want to." He was silent for several seconds, his hand moving to smooth back her hair, to trail down her throat. Surely, Sloan thought, he must feel the terrible pounding of her heart in the erratic racing of her pulse.

"Do you want to make love, Sloan?"

His voice, threading through the night like deep velvet, was husky and wistful. It was the perfect touch to break her final grasp on control. Sloan lay still just seconds, her eyes closing, her fingers clawing into fists at her side. Then she turned into him, her face burrowing into the dark hair on his chest, the tenseness of her body evaporating as she melded to him, her hands freed from their convulsive grasp to tremble as they rose to his shoulders, sweetly relishing the power play of muscles beneath them. "Yes," she whispered, barely audibly, "yes, please. Wes, make love to me. . . ."

"Oh, God." She heard his groan, deep and guttural within his throat. His hands raked through her hair, his kisses rained upon her face, covering her eyelids, devouring her mouth, falling with reverence over her breasts as he rolled over her with a need as urgent and demanding as she could have possibly desired. "Oh, dear God, wife," he murmured, divesting her gently of the silken sheath of nightgown that barely separated them. "I've missed you . . . wanted you, dreamed of you . . . making love to you . . ."

Sloan's shivers of agonized thirst slowly abated as he filled her with his heat, making love to her with a gentle trembling thoroughness that proved the truth of his words. Beneath the assault of hands and lips that enticed and seduced while they commanded and took, she came alive as she had never been before, craving release from her consuming madness, but savoring each touch of hungry lips upon her, lips that bruised her breasts, her thighs, sending lightning streaks of electric excitement ever closer to the core of her need. Nor could she fill herself with the taste and touch of him, drowning deeper and deeper in sensation as he rumbled groans of the pleasure she gave him.

He burst within her and she was filled, so sweetly gratified that she was at peace, realizing only then how sorely empty she had been. And he whispered softly that he loved her, and she clung to the words because she wanted more than anything to believe them.

Wes did mean his ardent whispers, uttered with passion in the dark because he was afraid to face them by day. Her sighs of pleasure made him tremble. The darkness had hidden the shattering joy in his eyes when she had come to him . . . a humble joy . . . his wife was perfection . . . a potion that slipped into the blood and intoxicated for life.

There was so much he wanted to say to her. He wanted her to know how sorry he really was, but it could never be explained, only felt.

And he couldn't explain anyway. She had taken him so easily once, cut him to the bone. She had the power to destroy him; he couldn't let her do it a second time. He couldn't talk to her as he wanted, until he could begin to believe, until time healed. They were wary opponents, ever circling . . .

He couldn't even assure himself that insecurity would keep him from striking out again . . . But now, as he held her close in the darkness, they had precious moments of mutual need . . . and caring. The battle tactics were out of the bedroom. Here he could love her.

And he did.

All through the night. He tooked what was his and cherished it, knowing morning could bring dissension and inevitably the light of day. Here, in the shadows, he could even accept her tentative whispers of love in return as the lazy comfort of satiation held them both in a spell and he cradled her to his form, softly stroking her hair.

"I do love you, Wes," she murmured softly against him, her voice so hesitant, so beseeching, that it hurt and he stiffened. Very, very faintly, he thought he heard a muffled sob.

"I love you," he said quietly. "But I don't trust you, Sloan."

"Then where do we go from here?" she murmured bleakly.

He was silent for a long time, but he continued to stroke her hair gently. "Trust is something that has to be earned," he said very softly, and fell back to silence.

Dawn was streaking through the windows, dispelling the guardian shadows of darkness, when they both slept, held together by the first tenuous thread of communication.

Wes was grateful that he held her in his arms against him, but his sleep was still not content or easy. He still had to wonder if she didn't wish that she slept with another man, a man she had also called husband and formed a relationship with that was her dream of near perfection. . . .

And he had to wonder if she really loved him, or if she still gave her love only to the ghost who remained in her dream.

She was a wonderful actress. He had learned that already. She could be protesting love for the mere convenience of saving the wealth she had plotted to obtain. . . .

Thank God she didn't know that any further acting was unnecessary. He loved and needed her so desperately that he would stay with her, give her anything in his power, no matter how she felt, just as long as he could be with her. . . .

# CHAPTER TEN

"What in hell are you doing?"

Wesley's voice, rasping over her shoulder, startled Sloan so badly that the pill she had been about to take flew from her hand and sailed into the kitchen sink. Whirling to face her husband, she stated the obvious with confusion. "I'm taking a pill." He stared at her stonily for a moment, his arms crossed over the white terry of his robe, then brushed her aside to pick up the packet she had left on the table. Very deliberately, he punched each pill from its plastic socket and flung them down the drain, one by one.

"What in hell are *you* doing?" Sloan demanded, astounded by his behavior. She had left him peacefully sleeping, confidently believing that the ardent lover of the night would awaken in a decent, if not loving, frame of mind. But he didn't appear to be in a "decent" mood at all. The tension in his sinewed body that she was learning to read so well was all too apparent. She wasn't sure how, but she had seriously angered him. "Wesley," she repeated more softly, "what are you doing? I need those." Had the man gone mad?

The last pill swirled down the drain, and Wesley tossed the packet into the garbage bag beneath the sink. "Where's your purse?" he demanded.

"Why?"

"I want the rest of these."

"There aren't any 'rest.' I get them each month." Sloan planted her hands on her hips and added crossly, "Except now I'll have to run by today and replace what you just threw away. What in God's name did you think you were doing? Did you think they were some type of drug —"

"I knew exactly what they were," Wes said irritably. "And you have a hell of a nerve taking the damn things without first discussing it with me."

"*What?*" Sloan's exclamation of amazement was a shrill cry.

"You heard me," Wesley snapped. Sloan could do nothing but stare at him, working her jaw, but still unable to offer a suitably scathing comeback. He returned her stare with challenging eyes, then turned to the automatic percolator. "Have you made coffee?"

"I've made coffee," Sloan retorted blandly, energizing herself into action to tug on the sleeve of his robe. "Would you mind explaining your childish actions? What difference does it make to you whether or not I take pills? I would think you'd appreciate —"

"Well, I don't," he cut through her speech. "I told you last night I'd thought of something I could get out of our bargain." He poured coffee into a cup and began to sip it black, his eyes implacably on her.

Again, Sloan was stunned speechless. She blinked, swallowed, and sputtered before managing, "You want me to . . . to . . ."

"Conceive," Wesley supplied, calmly drinking has coffee. "Yes. That is the usual way to have a child."

"You want a child," Sloan echoed numbly.

"My, what astounding comprehension!" Wesley drawled mockingly. "Yes, I want a child. That, my love, is something I can get out of this, something I've always wanted. I told you last night that I had decided there was a benefit I might derive."

"I know you told me," Sloan mumbled, automatically reaching for the coffeepot to occupy her trembling hands, "but I thought . . . I thought . . . that you meant . . ."

"Let me help you with that," Wes said,

amused by her confusion. He took the coffeepot from her hands and poured the steaming brew into a cup. He placed the cup firmly into her grip, then leaned nonchalantly back on the counter. "You thought that I had decided on your lovely person as sufficient payment for a . . . loveless . . . marriage." Sloan felt her skin begin to heat beneath his cool appraisal and choked as she sipped a burning gulp. Wes patted her on the back, laughing at her obvious discomfiture. "Darling wife," he remarked with a small shake of his head, "you are so easy to read. That is exactly what you thought. Sorry — you were wrong." His cool green gaze raked her mirthfully from head to toe. "Not that I don't find your charms intricately pleasing, but in all honest reality, they are available elsewhere."

Sloan's hand rose automatically to slap his devilishly leering face and hopefully wipe the amused grin clean from it. But this time Wesley anticipated her action, catching her arm and salvaging her cup simultaneously. "Don't!" he warned imperiously, twisting her wrist until a small cry escaped her. His grip eased, but he continued to hold her wrist and his jaw was rigidly set. "Lady, you will learn to control those violent little impulses of yours. Lash out at me again and you'll be very sorry."

Sloan clamped her teeth together and glared into his eyes defiantly, tilting her head with regal pride. He wouldn't dare! Still . . . she might be wiser to learn to cut him with words as he did her. Her arm went limp within his grasp. "Perhaps, if you could learn to curb your tongue, Mr. Adams," she challenged coldly, "I could learn to control my violent impulses.

"And if you expect a child," she snapped, "you'd better start being a little nicer to its prospective mother."

Wesley's eyes flashed, and he dug his fingers into her shoulders to pull her against his heat-radiating length. "Is that a bribe or a threat?" he asked, but oddly, his voice held no menace. Something that belied his mockery was behind the question . . . tenderness?

Sloan's head fell as she shivered, and she buried it into his shoulder. "Neither," was her muffled reply. He had taken her by surprise at first, even appalled her with the suggestion of a child. But she suddenly wanted his baby very much. She loved children, and Wesley had already proved himself an excellent father with the sons and daughter of another man. He had every right in the world to a child of his own.

There was only one problem. The thought of two A.M. feedings again didn't bother her, nor did the idea of diapers or the demanding attention needed by an infant. The problem was Wesley. She loved him, ached for him with her entire being. Yet, how could she bear his child when she knew his love for her had died along with his trust and respect?

Trust had to be earned, he had told her, and it might be a long road to winning back his trust. But as he began to stroke her hair gently as her head lay against his chest, she knew she was willing to traverse that long road.

"Would you like a fourth child, Sloan?" Wes asked her softly.

She nodded, not trusting herself to speak.

"Be sure," he said carefully. "I wouldn't force you to have a child against your will. I'd rather you be honest with me than run behind my back and pick up another package of those pills."

"I am being honest," Sloan said, talking to his chest. "But would you . . ."

"Would I what?"

"Would you mind telling me where you've been for the past month?" Sloan intended her question to be bold and challenging, but

275

fear of the possible answer added a note of pique.

Wesley laughed easily, annoying her to the core. "You mean who have I been with, don't you?"

"You know exactly what I mean!" Sloan snapped, pulling abruptly away from him to stomp across the kitchen. He had the exasperating habit of making her want to claw his eyes out, and she was desperately trying to avoid such useless behavior.

"I was in Paris for two weeks," Wes said, straightening and ambling slowly after her. "And since then I've been in Kentucky. In fact," he mused, planting hands on her shoulders while a rakish grin settled subtly into the corners of his mouth, "that's where I came up with my idea." He held her at arm's length and studied her with teasing appraisal. "One of my mares just produced her third colt, a magnificent animal, like the ones before him. The mare is a born breeder. Just like you, my sweet. I'm sure to get a healthy, beautiful child."

Sloan felt as if she were strangling. Blood suffused ringingly into her head with fury. "A brood mare!" she hissed, shaking his hands from her shoulders. "A brood mare!" her voice rose shrilly. "That's what you think of me!" Her wrath was causing her

276

teeth to shatter. "That's just marvelous, Wes. Just marvelous! Suppose we have this child? What happens then?"

"Then we see," he said softly.

He wasn't fast enough to catch her hand when it flew across his face that time, and she had whirled away from him while the stinging sensation still seeped into his stunned cheek. "Go back to Paris, Wes!" she called over her shoulder as she stalked down the hall. Aware that he had made a mess of the whole thing and willing to apologize, to try to explain . . . "Sloan!" he called again, more sharply.

She made no reply, and he heard the lock click in the bedroom.

"Dammit!" he roared, his apology dying in his throat as she ignored him. He followed her down the hall. "Sloan, I'm talking to you! Open the damned door!"

He didn't ask a second time; the door gave with a single lunge of his shoulder, and Sloan, seated on the bed in a dejected huddle, straightened with wide eyes as she met the thunder of his face, features as harsh and stormy as if he were about to meet the defensive line of the Green Bay Packers.

"Get away from me!" she hissed, startled and frightened. She hadn't ignored him on purpose; she had been so preoccupied with her inner dilemma that she had really closed out everything. She jumped as he approached her, attempting to elude him but failing.

"Sloan," Wes tried to begin, clasping her upper arms.

She had no conception that he was still trying to apologize; she was sure from his face that his intent was dangerous, and she flailed against him heedlessly. "Sloan —" he tried once more, but at that moment her flying fingers raked against his chest, the nails clawing, creating rising welts.

They both stood stock-still, Sloan with horror, Wes closing his eyes and clamping down hard on his jaw, shaking as he tried to breathe easily and leash the steam rising within him.

"Oh, Lord, Wes, I'm sorry!" Sloan cried.

"Damn, you have a vile temper!" he muttered, opening his eyes. She was gazing up at him with eyes of liquid sapphire, naked and beautiful with remorse. The hands that held her drew her into him, and he smelled the sweet scent of her wild hair. He brushed her forehead with a kiss, lifted her chin with a finger, and kissed her lips with a hungry intensity.

"What are you doing," she asked breathlessly as they broke, and he lifted her into his arms, cradling her to warm, sinewed muscles.

"Well," he murmured, "my first impulse was to wring your lovely little neck. I could do that. Or I could make love to you . . ."

"You're crazy. . . ."

"Yes."

It was a tempest, a reckless soaring into foaming rapids, riding crest after crest, twirling, whirling, crashing, rebounding.

Yet temper brought no ruthlessness. Wes harbored her, cherished her, swept her into the glory of his wild winds.

She should have denied him.

He had made his opinion of her so very clear.

But she held on to her love, clinging to the belief that no man could be so gentle and tender against such odds if there wasn't truth to his love.

It was a matter of truth. . . .

And learning. . . .

And if loving was part of that trust, then she was right to love. But did any reasoning matter? He touched her, and it didn't matter. But it should matter. . . . She should have the strength to insist that they have more than the consuming physical need. . . .

She didn't have the strength . . . only the

need. Only the desire to believe the cherishing, bend to the storm . . . be there as he was with her when they soared over the fall, gently guiding her to the still waters beneath. . . .

Where she turned from him and curled into a little ball of solitude, bewildered and confused.

She couldn't understand her own behavior, much less begin to comprehend his. They could reach the borderline of friendship, and then all was lost with a reckless word or deed. Then they were mortal combatants, then the most tender and passionate of lovers.

But when it was over, they were on the defensive again. And it would be hard to go back and see just what had triggered what. . . .

"Sloan."

A quality in his tone compelled her to look his way, but she stubbornly denied herself. With obstinate willpower she kept her head in her pillow.

"What?"

"Look at me," he persisted with firm patience.

She turned slowly, wincing as she realized that countless muscles were sore. If his mood were similar to the one that had precipitated the broken door, she reasoned with herself, it would be plain old stupid to disobey his soft-spoken order.

His head rested in his hands, and his eyes were on the ceiling, seeming strangely to reflect her own emotions. As she watched him, his gaze riveted sideways to her.

"I never mean to hurt you," he said quietly.

"You didn't hurt me." She frowned, adding bitterly, "You know you didn't." She winced at the sight of the scratches she had inflicted. "I hurt you."

He grunted impatiently and leaned over on his elbow to face her. "That's not what I mean. I acted without thinking — or discussing, rather. I said things in haste, and although I was teasing you about the mare bit, I'll admit I was crude." He smiled ruefully. "I was scared."

"What?" Sloan whispered incredulously.

"You might have turned me down," he said flatly.

"Oh!" Sloan murmured, shocked that it meant so much to him.

"I goad you a lot, Sloan, and I'm usually quickly sorry," Wes continued, "but still too late. We all say things in anger, and the problem is that they can't be taken back. If I could undo half the pain I caused you in Belgium, I gladly would. But I was hurt, Sloan, and that hurt was like a knife wound in the back that made me angrier than I've ever been in my life. You can't imagine how I felt to reach your house and find you telling your sister how you had planned to marry me for my money. It was crippling, I had never felt so used and betrayed. . . . I planned to surprise you with a kiss and instead I got the surprise. I slammed the door because I couldn't stand to hear any more of it. . . . Damn, Sloan," he muttered fiercely, running a knuckle down the length of her arm, "I really wanted to throttle you that night. I had to leave . . . and then, I still had to have you, but I had to let you know too that I was well aware of your motives."

"Oh, God, Wes," Sloan moaned, longing to reach out and touch his cheek with its slightly rough edge of overnight shadow, but rubbing her own temple instead. "I'd give anything to take back that night — you only heard half a conversation. It was true, but it wasn't true . . . and I can't take any of it back or undo it. . . ." she trailed miserably.

He was silent for a minute, then shifted so that he was sitting to draw her head against his side and take on the task of rubbing her forehead himself. When he spoke again, it

282

was with the thread of silk she loved.

"I don't want to spend my days in constant battle. We have major problems, but I don't want a divorce. I don't believe that you do either — especially not while you're still financing that new dance school of yours."

"Wes . . ." Sloan implored.

"Sorry, I was doing it again." Wes grinned ruefully. "But we are going to set down a few ground rules. Legitimate deals. I promise no more wisecracks, and you promise to control your temper — no more slaps. I won't go anywhere without your knowing exactly where I am — and we both make a pact to say what we really mean instead of striking out below the belt when we're bothered. And please, no more businesses that I know nothing about! How about it?" His soothing fingers moved from her temples to tug gently at the ends of her hair.

Sloan nodded slowly. "Wesley," she said, biting down on her lip. "You *didn't* hear the whole conversation. I told Cassie that night that I did love you . . . had loved you. . . ." Taking a deep breath, Sloan tried to explain the whole thing. "Cassie came over that night because she didn't want me marrying you because she was afraid it would be a disaster. She knew I wasn't crazy about seeing you in the first place, and then things moved so fast. . . . She is my sister, but she thinks the world of you. . . .'' Sloan lamely sought the right words. "I was trying to tell her the truth — that yes, at first the money had been the draw, but only at the very first. I had no idea that you had heard any of the conversation, but when you left, I really didn't need to explain any further to her! She knew that I loved you, really loved you. . . .'' Again, her voice trailed away feebly. "I won't suggest that you just ask Cassie," she started again with quiet dignity. "I realize that she is still *my* sister — and that you could well imagine I've had plenty of time to warn her that you heard what we were saying. . . . I can understand that . . . but, God, Wes, it is the truth! I did love you, and I did tell her that night. . . . I wish you would believe that!"

"It should be very easy to try," Wes said softly in sincere promise, "because I want to."

It was a qualifying statement, but a start. Sloan buried her face into his shoulder. They had been ripping one another apart when they were really after the same things. "Wes?" She could let matters lie, maybe should let matters lie . . .

But then she couldn't . . . she had to ask. . . .

"I spent two rotten weeks in Paris by my-self," he said, anticipating her question. "and since then, I was in Kentucky. Alone." His touch was gentle as he smoothed her wild hair. "I haven't been near another woman since the night I first walked into your house. Does that answer your question?"

She nodded mutely against his chest.

"And do you believe me?"

"I — I think," she faltered, thrown by the question. "I want to believe you —"

"Don't you see?" Wes queried lightly. "That's the point." His voice became passionate and intense as he groaned, "I want to believe you. I want to trust you more than anything in the world. . . ."

"But I do love you, Wes," Sloan choked, burying deeper into his side. "I did need money, everything was going so badly, but I never meant to be . . . mercenary. Your love was like a dream come true, and then I knew that I loved you, too. Then, and, I do love you now, Wes!"

"That is what I want most to believe," Wes said, his voice a soft whisper again. "And I am trying to. It just takes time for wounds to heal. We need that time."

They both fell silent, but it was a comfortable, restful silence. For the first time, they were totally at peace in one another's company.

It was Sloan, who, growing drowsy, finally broke the bond of quiet. Resting her chin on his chest, she looked into his eyes, determined to take a further step on the new road to open honesty.

"I do want your baby, Wes," she told him wistfully.

His arms tightened around her, and his reply was one of the most tender she had ever heard. "Thank you."

# CHAPTER ELEVEN

Things should have worked out simply from that point, Sloan thought; they were capable of talking, capable of breaking across the barriers of mistrust.

But talking didn't necessarily mean that the past could be erased, and although their relationship had become pleasant and cordial in the week of Wesley's return, she knew that they both still held back, both clung to a measure of reserve.

They had hurt each other, and she supposed it only natural that they both still wear armor when treading upon the soft ground of one another's feelings.

It was therefore with a little unease the following Friday night after the children had long been asleep and Florence too had retired that Sloan sought Wes out in the den that he had turned into a pseudo-office.

She had had visions of the scene, played it a million ways. And in all her visions, it had been beautiful. She had teased and tormented him, smiling while promising him a secret. She had played the feminine role to the hilt, insisting upon an elegant dinner out before allowing her secret to leave her lips. And Wes . . . well, of course, he had responded with all the joyous enthusiasm and tender care she could have desired. . . .

But when it came down to it, she was frightened. She could give him news that should surprise and elate him — news he wanted to hear. News that had thrilled her. But despite all of her happiness she was also filled with a heavy feeling of anxiety, almost a sadness. *We should have had more time,* she kept thinking. They should have had the time to keep talking, to break down the guards and barriers, to learn how to live and love together. . . .

But they didn't have the time. She had verified a slow dawning suspicion this morning, and although she could have waited to tell him, she didn't deem it fair. She had begun all that was wrong between them with a lie — withholding this information would seem to be as great a lie as the one she had used to play with his emotions in a time that now seemed interminably long ago.

Besides, she couldn't have held back any longer. Despite the shaky foundation of their marriage, she was hesitantly glowing. Deep inside she was thrilled and smug with herself — already madly in love with and protective of his child. She had to share the baby's existence. . . .

And yet it didn't go a bit as she had envisioned in her daydreams — hindsight would tell her it was her own fault, but as she approached Wes that night, she wasn't privy to hindsight. She was nervous, and afraid. From this point on, she would never really know if Wes had forgiven her completely, or if he was merely satisfied with his end of the bargain.

Her voice was consequently sharp when she stood in the doorway, her throat constricting as she watched his dark head bent over his papers, his attention fully on his work. "Wes."

He glanced up at her, his eyes registering both surprise and annoyance at her tone. "Yes?" He didn't snap at her; he was polite but aloof. That was about all that could be said for the week, Sloan thought dryly — polite and aloof. He was determined not to argue with her, determined not to bring up the past. They communicated just fine in the bedroom at night with the lights off, but in the morning the wary remoteness was back. Sloan began to wish he would yell or scream or argue — anything to dislodge that invisible shield that still kept them apart.

"I have to talk to you," she announced, once more wincing at her own tone. She wanted so badly to be natural, to share the enthusiasm she was feeling. . . .

"Come in." He pushed back from the desk and indicated the wingback chair a few feet across from it. "What is it?"

Settling into the chair, Sloan knew her chance to change the cool tide of the conversation had come. All she had to do was put warmth into her abrupt tone, let her feelings show. . . .

But it was as if she had lost voluntary control of her actions. She didn't tease, she didn't torment, she didn't leave the chair and force herself into his lap, curling her arms around his neck, as she longed to do. She blurted her information almost brusquely.

"You're getting your part of the bargain, Wes. I'm pregnant."

A barrage of emotions flashed through his eyes in less than seconds — then they were guarded, opaque. His dark lashes swept over them, and Sloan suddenly felt as if she were facing a stranger.

"Are you sure?" His brows were knitting into a frown. "I didn't think it was possible to know so quickly —"

"It isn't quickly," Sloan interrupted, feeling a flush steal over her face. Absurd that she could still blush in front of him, after all they had shared. But what she had to say went back to Belgium, a time when she would have doubted they could have even come to this strange, touching-but-not-touching existence. Her own lashes fell over her eyes. "I conceived on our . . . honeymoon." She didn't mean it to sound bitter, she really didn't — but it did.

Wes was silent for a long time. So long that she began to think he didn't care anymore, that his request of a week ago had merely been another way to taunt her. . . . But no, she didn't believe that; Wes had been too sincere when they did speak. He was honest with her. He did love her; she knew that and clung to it — even as she knew through his admission that it would take time for him to trust her.

She couldn't know that he was silent because he was busy berating himself. A child, their child, and she was offering the wonderful information as part of a "bargain." Because of him. Because he had come back so determined to keep her, and weld her to him, that he had forced her to do so. What a damned idiot he had been — it was almost as if fate laughed at him. If he had said nothing . . . if he hadn't come upon her like a bear . . . she might be coming to him differently now. She might have come into the room full of the joy and enthusiasm . . . He never needed to force her into a bargain . . . she had been pregnant with his child at the time. . . .

"Are you sure?" he asked huskily.

"Positive," she answered, still afraid to risk a meeting with those opaque eyes again. But he was going to force the issue.

"Sloan, look at me."

She did so finally, hands clasped tightly on her lap, her posture rigid with tension.

"Are you happy?" he asked softly.

Her nod was jerky; she could feel tears hovering behind her eyes and bit down hard on her inner lip to prevent them. "Are you?" she managed to ask.

He stood with an easy movement and made his way around the desk, his eyes never leaving hers. And then the opaqueness was gone; he was kneeling down beside her, taking her quivering hands into his. She glanced at him, suddenly feeling the tears drip down her face as he finally replied, "I'm not happy, my love, I'm ecstatic. That is, if you are."

. Sloan nodded as he touched her cheeks,

brushing away the dampness with a gentle finger.

"Why are you crying?" he demanded gently.

Sloan shook her head; she couldn't explain. "Because I'm pregnant, I guess," she told him, star sapphires seeming to gleam in eyes that were wide and liquid. She didn't realize that she now looked to him with ardent appeal — and an aching need. "Women are supposed to be highly emotional at this time, didn't you know?"

He chuckled. "So I've heard." His voice went very low in answer to her appeal. "I don't mind 'emotional' at all, just as long as you are happy beneath it. I love you, Sloan."

Suddenly she felt as if the barriers were gone — she hadn't erased mistrust, but she was comfortable in the belief that Wes was trying, that his love was great enough to eradicate the mistakes they had both made in the past.

"I love you, Wes," she echoed, eyes beseeching that he believe her. She was always so afraid to say those three little words.

He didn't dispute her. Very tenderly he kissed her hands, then her forehead, then abruptly and with far less tenderness, he plucked her from the chair and into his arms, laughing at the startled expression that replaced her tears.

"My darling," he explained, heading through the den door, "you came in like a prisoner of war to give me the most marvelous news of my life. Then you start weeping all over me! This, Mrs. Adams, is a time for celebration. We've a bottle of Asti Spumanti in the back of the fridge, and we're going to toast one another to death. Hmmmmm . . . maybe I'll do the majority of the toasting. . . . I don't believe you should be drinking too much. . . ."

Sloan's tears were changing to giddy laughter. "I can certainly have a glass of champagne!" she protested. "You forget, I'm an old hand at this."

"Well, I'm not," Wes protested. "And so you are going to follow all the rules. You don't smoke, that's good, and we can hire a teacher to work with Jim —"

"Hey!" Sloan protested, laughing as she was deposited on the kitchen counter while he prodded through the refrigerator. "I'm not going to stop dancing — I don't have to, Wesley, really. I danced professionally until I was five months along with both Jamie and Laura."

Wes stopped his prowling for a moment to gaze her way with stern eyes. "I don't like it, Sloan. You're ten pounds slimmer than you should be to begin with; you've been taking pills —" He halted abruptly; his stare seeming to narrow and bore into her. "Sloan," he said tensely, "why were you taking those pills so long?"

"Because I didn't know, Wesley," she explained quickly. Oh God, she thought mournfully, could he really believe that she would try to lose his child? "I'm afraid I've never known for quite some time." She was blushing again; how ridiculous. "I didn't even suspect until Monday morning, and probably only then because we had been talking. . . ." How lame she sounded. "But it's all right, Wes, really it is. Many women take pills accidentally, and, and, nothing happens."

His gaze softened. "You really do want this baby?"

"Yes." She kept her eyes level with his. "I told you that I did, and I mean that, Wes." She didn't tell him how good it felt, how wonderful to cherish and nourish his child within her.

"All right," he said gruffly, "you can keep teaching then — for a while — but we won't stretch it too far. And you can have one glass of Asti Spumanti." His eyes had taken on a twinkle, and she felt like crying again with relief. Things were going to be all right.

Then she was in his arms again, laughing as he stuffed the cold bottle and two crystal glasses into her hands so that he could carry her.

"What about your work?" she demanded as he booted open the door to their bedroom.

"It won't go anywhere," he promised gravely. And then the door was being slammed behind them, and she was laughing while he undressed her. She still attempted to hold the champagne and glasses and feel the inevitable warmth and sensual stimulation steal over her with his commanding touch. . . .

Things *were* going to be all right.

And they were all right. Wes started coming into the studio with her, telling her he was looking at books, but she was sure he was watching over her.

She didn't mind the feeling.

In fact, the only spur in her existence was an uneasy feeling in the back of her mind which she usually managed to ignore. Wes had been back in Gettysburg for two full weeks, and he hadn't mentioned a thing about Kentucky. She knew he hadn't decided to remain in the north indefinitely — his business holdings outside of Louisville were too vast for him to suddenly forget them. She also knew that he loved his home, his work, and the prestigious empire he and his brother had created together. She was aware that he would have to be going back — but he made no reference to her going with him. She should bring it up, she told herself, but she was loath to do so. She didn't dare do a thing to mar the happiness the announcement of the child had brought them both. As long as things were moving along so very comfortably, she couldn't dare make a change that might be disastrous. She was also still afraid of answers she might receive if she questioned too closely. She didn't want to take a chance on hearing that their marriage was still on a trial basis — not complete until she had actually delivered the child Wes craved.

In that respect, she wasn't frightened. She had three beautiful children — even Terry, born early in the midst of grief and shock, had clung tenaciously to life and health.

They were becoming a rounded family, and Sloan loved becoming that family in all the simple ways. Sharing dinners, watching television, planning their time. The money that Sloan had once longed for now meant so little. Her pleasure was in the man — watching him help Jamie with projects, chastising Laura while still treating her like a little princess, taking Terry with his toddling precociousness beneath his own wing. As it had always been with him, what was hers was his. No blood brother could have been better to Cassie, more companionable to George.

If only she didn't carry that edge of nervousness over his refusal to bring up his own life, and the home far away. . . .

It was two and half weeks after his return that the bomb dropped. It was late, near midnight, and she was comfortably curled to Wes's side as they both read paperbacks, when the phone rang. Their mutually curious expressions as Wes picked up the phone signified a loss at who could be calling so late.

Curious, Sloan's raised brows knit into a frown. After Wes's initial "Hello," he went silent, listening, as seemingly countless seconds ticked by. Then his reply was a brief "Hold on a minute." Handing the receiver to Sloan, he slipped from the bed and into his robe. "Hang that up for me, will you please? I'm going to take it in the den."

Not waiting for her acknowledgment, he exited the room. Sloan was glad he didn't turn around — he would have seen her jaw drop and her eyes widen with startled pain.

He had just dismissed her as nothing more than a personal secretary — not trusting her, and not caring that she was worried. . . .

But then Wes had the sure capability of turning from ardent lover to cold stranger — hard stranger — in a matter of seconds.

Staring bleakly after him, Sloan eyed the receiver she held. Temptation was overwhelming, because her pride had been wounded. She had a right to know what was going on in her home at midnight. She was, after all, Wesley's wife. . . .

Sloan brought the receiver to her ear just in time to hear Wes pick up downstairs. She intended to announce herself, but he began to speak immediately. "Okay, Dave, I'm here. I can get there immediately; I picked up a little jet the other day. In the meantime, call Doc Jennings — I don't care what you have to do to find him or what you have to take him away from. If our entire stock is down —" Wes's voice didn't fade away; it stopped abruptly. She was startled by his tone becoming as curt and precise as an icicle, although, because of his brother's hearing of his words miles away, he did couch his request politely. "Sloan — I have it down here, thank you. You may hang up now."

"Hey, Sloan," Dave cut in cheerfully.

"Didn't know you were there. How are you?"

"Fine, thanks, Dave," Sloan murmured quickly, feeling as if her face had gone afire. She mumbled a good-bye and set the receiver hastily into its cradle, wondering with bleak but increasing anger how Wes could have managed to be so curt, so icy cold, to her. And then she realized that he had left the room purposely so that she would not hear his plans — his full intention had been to shut her out. . . .

Alternating between the despairing realization that nothing had really changed — Wes trusted her less than one of his well-nurtured horses and had no intention of sharing his life with her, even if he did humor her and join into hers — and the infuriating proof that he would continue to do what he pleased with no regard to her feelings, Sloan sank into the bed, her limbs also torn between racing heat and numbness.

He was leaving; he was going to Kentucky. And he was leaving in a plane he had purchased — and neglected to mention to her.

And on top of all that, he would shortly come stalking back up to the room to coldly denounce her as an eavesdropper, condemning her with that oceanic stare that was like a razor's edge. . . .

The hell he will, she decided grimly, slipping from the bed in his wake. For a moment her body protested her movement; her stomach, always a little queasy in her first months of pregnancy, wavered out a warning signal. Sloan ignored it; she was never truly nauseated, and her decision was taking precedence. She was going to challenge Wes with all the wrath she could muster before he hit her with his icy disdain.

Donning her robe and sliding into her slippers, she followed his trail to the den with equal determination. When she entered, he was just hanging up the phone, appearing ridiculously dignified and coolly authoritative for a man with tousled black hair clad in a velour robe. His eyes, in fact, chilled her; they brought her back in time to a cool morning in Belgium when she learned she had indeed pulled upon a tiger's tail. . . .

"Ahhh, my wife," he murmured, "the eavesdropper."

Sloan flushed but refused to be intimidated. "Sometimes eavesdroppers hear what they should have been told in the first place."

His shrug seemed to be another dismissal. "Obviously, you would have been told. I'm leaving tonight. I did assume that you would notice when I packed." Why was he snapping at her? Wes wondered. He knew the answer; he didn't like to admit it to himself. He was afraid that she wouldn't notice, not really notice. She responded to him, she professed to love him, she was charming, she was his — everything he had loved all those years — everything he had planned on having — prayed to have — since that day he had watched her. He didn't covet her as another man's wife; he had only come to that when he knew she was alone and yearned to alleviate her pain.

And now he wondered if he had ever come to do so. She wanted the baby — badly — he believed. But Sloan loved children. And the baby had been conceived long ago. . . .

He wasn't prone to insecurity, but he was uncontrollably insecure now. He didn't believe that she intended to leave him, but he still wondered if she didn't close her eyes at night and envision him as another man. . . .

Wes watched now as stunned hurt filled her eyes before she could shade them, and he was ready to kick himself. "I'm sorry," he apologized gruffly. "But I don't appreciate your listening in on a private conversation. I wanted the facts first so that I could tell you how long I would be gone."

"How long will you be gone?" she asked hollowly. Did she care, Wes asked himself desperately. As long as she was left with provisions and memories, did she really care. He heard hauntings of her soft voice telling him she loved him, but he had heard it before when it had been false.

"About two weeks," he replied curtly.

"You're flying yourself out?" Again, her voice had that hollowed sound, curiously strained.

"Yes," he replied impatiently. "If I were to keep driving all the time, I'd spend half the time on the road."

"Wes" — was there a note of anguish in her voice? — "you didn't tell me you had purchased a plane. You never even told me that you were a pilot."

"I'm not a pilot. I have my pilot's license."

"Wes" — her voice was definitely rising shrilly — "don't you think we should have discussed it?"

Stupidly, he didn't realize what she was getting at. "I can afford the plane, I assure you. I don't remember you discussing the setup of an entire business with me."

He heard the sharp intake of her breath; something sizzled into her sapphire eyes. "Wes, you seem to have forgotten I've lost one husband in those little planes." She turned away from him suddenly. "But suit yourself."

God, she could sound cold. He wanted to tell her that he was sorry, but he felt the terrible chill of her demeanor. "Cheer up," he heard himself saying. "Since you're planning my demise, I'll remind you that you'll be a very rich widow this time." He saw the heave of her shoulders and suddenly hated himself with a black passion. Belatedly, words of apology came to his lips, and his strides were eating the distance between them. "Sloan," she tried to shake off the restraining hands on her shoulders and look away, but he wouldn't allow her. Fighting back tears, she met his eyes rebelliously. "Sloan," he persisted softly, "I'm sorry. Yes, Terry died in a plane crash. But millions have died on the highways. I'm a very good pilot. I'll be safer in the sky than I would be in a car."

He could feel her shaking; she knew it. It would be impossible for him not to feel her trembling as he held her. But somehow, she couldn't reply to him. "Sloan," he insisted tensely, "answer me."

Bleak, liquid eyes lifted to his; the indifferent tone was back in her voice. "What do I say?" she asked. "You're flying out tonight; you'll be gone two weeks. It's settled."

Yes, it was settled. Her opinion didn't matter. He had apologized, but he hadn't changed a thing. Even his apology, she was sure, had been issued because he had seen her wince with the sudden tension in her lower back. It was frightfully apparent that he didn't want her upset. But then that, of course, was because of the baby. And it didn't seem to occur to him that she could tolerate the plane — even happily board it — if only he wanted her with him. . . .

He exhaled a long sigh. "Go on back to bed, Sloan; you're shivering, and you need to get to sleep. I have a few things to get together down here, and I won't need to pack much, so I shouldn't disturb you."

That was it — a dismissal. He was leaving. Sloan nodded dispiritedly and turned away as he released her. "Sloan." She heard a slight catch in his voice and turned back. "It might be nice if you kissed me good-bye."

He took her in his arms before she could have a chance to refuse him, and his mouth claimed hers with a bittersweet combination of persuasiveness and demand. Unable to resist him, Sloan felt herself melt to his touch, knowing it would be denied her for what would seem an eternity. She arched herself against the warm strength of his frame, hungrily met his thrusting tongue with her own. And then she felt the salt of tears on her cheek and disentangled herself, turning away before he could see them. Saying nothing else, she quit the room.

The encounter had left her absurdly weak. Returning to the bedroom with her thoughts in a turmoil, she at first ignored the pain in her back that was proving to be persistent. Wesley didn't want her in his home. He was leaving for two weeks, but she had no guarantee that he meant to return at that time. He could leave, and find himself busy, and not care if he hurried back to a wife he didn't trust.

Of course, he would be back eventually. He wanted to see his child. . . .

The next stab of pain she felt was so shocking that it ripped her cruelly from her mental dilemma and sent her staggering to the bedpost for support. Stunned, she held on as the pain continued to rack through her. In disbelief she thought she had felt nothing so horrendously unbearable since Terry's birth.

It was then that she started to scream Wesley's name in a long low wail of agony and terror.

Her cry jolted him with panic as nothing ever had before in his life. Wes bolted from the den and made it to the bedroom as if jet-propelled. At first he couldn't ferret out what had happened. Sloan was doubled over on the floor, her slender hands losing their grip on the bedpost. He took a step nearer, and it felt as if his heart sank cleanly from him; he held his breath. She was saturated in blood. So much blood. How could it possibly have come from such a wraithlike figure? How could she possibly have any left to pulse through her veins, to keep her heart beating . . . ?

He was galvanized into desperate action, knowing even as he shook as if palsied that he had to move quickly. He was shouting as he scooped her into his arms, loud enough to raise even Florence, and then he was issuing curt commands to the frightened but alert housekeeper. She was dialing the hospital even as he was slipping Sloan into the car, loath to take a chance on wasting the precious minutes to wait for the ambulance. She opened her eyes once; a weak, pained smile touched just the corners of her lips. "Wesley," she whispered, and then her sapphire eyes closed once again, and all color was gone from her ashen face.

My wife, he thought desperately. No, my life, my existence. . . .

And then he was careening toward the

hospital, her cheek resting against his knee. . . .

In actuality, he wasn't shut out long. But every second was an eternity. He paced the empty, sterile halls, praying.

And his mind would return to the nightmare. The grim look of her obstetrician — the man who had delivered not only her three children, but Sloan herself. A man who had made it to the hospital after Florence's call almost as quickly as he.

An older man, but obviously competent, obviously deeply caring for his pale, lifeless patient. A man who had assured Wes he wouldn't let her die as he wheeled her away.

But he had been worried. Wes had known he was worried. The sharp old eyes had taken in all the blood.

And so Wes kept pacing, a caged tiger stalking the relentless prison of his heart, fighting fear, cruelly cutting into himself with blame. There was the possibility that he might lose her — and it would be his fault. No, he hadn't been cruel to her, he hadn't misused her. He had even been what some might term a good husband since his return. But he knew what she had known — he had held back. He had denied her the security and faith that she had needed from him. . . . He had forced her to have the child . . . no, she had wanted the child . . . no, he derided himself fiercely, he had forced her; he could remember with stabbing clarity the way he had taken her in Belgium, the time the child very likely had been conceived . . . and even that had been all so unnecessary. He had known she didn't love him, but he had also known that she intended to remain his wife, to offer what she could.

But like a fool he had been insanely jealous of a ghost. If she made it, he swore, he wouldn't care. He would simply cherish her, be there, take care of her as he had longed to do since he first set eyes upon her gamin face and sapphire eyes.

No. He stopped his pacing and raised his eyes heavenward in a solemn vow, a strange figure, a virile giant in a bloodstained velour robe silently beseeching God.

I'll release her. I'll see that she never has another worry, another care, but I'll let her resume her life alone.

That was the state Cassie and George found him in. Cassie, already worried by Florence's call, saw the blood on Wesley's clothing and burst into frantic tears as she raced toward him.

Wes took one look at the panic and anguish on his sister-in-law's face and was suddenly sure that she knew something he didn't. He felt his breath leave him, his heartbeat waver. His world became the swirling mist of miserable gray he knew it would be without Sloan.

With an agonized cry that would rip apart the heart of anyone within hearing range, the virile giant crashed to the floor.

Consciousness came back to him with sharp severity which he strove to fight off. He didn't want to come back. But then he heard Cassie's voice, felt her touch.

"Wes, she's okay, she wants to see you. Wes!"

He opened his eyes. He hadn't been out long — he was still on the floor, his head dragged onto his sister-in-law's lap. Hovering above him were the faces of George and the doctor — both filled with relief, a relief that was slowly dawning to amusement.

"Your wife is going to be fine, Mr. Adams," the doctor was assuring him. His voice lowered. "You know, of course, that she has lost the baby, but she will be fine."

"Oh, God." His hands were shaking convulsively as he buried his face into them, oblivious, uncaring that his tears of relief and joy were damp on his cheeks.

"Wes," Cassie reminded him softly, "she

wants to see you." He stood up, her empathetic eyes still on him, and he found his strength within them. Squeezing her arm, he turned to rush down the corridor.

"Wait." George caught his arm and stuffed a large paper bag into his arms, his head inclined toward Wes's robe. "Florence told us you ran down here in your robe. I'm not so sure it would be good for her to see you looking like that."

Wes nodded his thanks with a brief, rueful smile, then directed his hasty steps for the bathroom to change. "We'll be here," Cassie called after him softly. "Tell her we'll see her as soon as we can in the morning."

"Five minutes only, Mr. Adams," the obstetrician called. "She needs rest now."

Wes nodded to them all, still dizzy with gratitude to the deity who had allowed her to live.

She was still under sedation, and the world was misty. But even while disbelief assailed her, the misery of truth was there. The tiny life that had been within her was gone. The baby was dead. Doc Ricter had tried to tell her that it wasn't her fault, that miscarriages were often a mystery, an act of God. But Sloan couldn't believe him. She had killed her own baby, she had been oblivious, she hadn't taken care. She had insisted on dancing. . . .

And it wasn't just her baby she had killed; it was Wes's. The baby he wanted so badly . . . the baby who had held them together, offered them hope . . .

She had asked for Wes because she had needed him. She hadn't been able to control her plea with the sedative making her weak. But as the seconds ticked by in her world of white, she knew she could no longer ask him to stay. Doc had severely warned her against trying again for quite some time. . . .

She had nothing left to offer him.

But suddenly he was standing in the doorway, paused for a second, and then he was at her side.

Her hand was enveloped within his large ones; he was on his knees. She could vaguely feel a dampness as he brought her fingers tenderly to his cheeks, and then to his lips.

"Wes," she whispered, trying to get the words out without choking on the ever-present tears, "I've lost the baby."

"I know, my love. I'm so sorry, so very sorry."

It was like Wes, she thought vaguely. Always so concerned for others first. She had to keep trying, she had to make him understand. "Wes, we . . . I may not be able to have another."

"Hush," he murmured, his fingers moving to brush back her damp hair. "It doesn't matter. Nothing matters. You're going to be all right and I'll never ask anything of you again; I'll see that you never want for anything. . . ."

Oh Lord, she thought sinkingly, he did want to be rid of her; he would care for her, pay her anything, to be free of her. . . .

"I . . . I don't want anything, Wes," she murmured miserably. "I'm going to release you so that you can have your child for sure. . . ." She simply hadn't the strength to prevent them. In anguished silence the tears began to cascade down her face.

"Child?" he was awash with confusion, not daring to believe what was staring him in the face. "Oh, dear God, Sloan! I don't care if I ever father a child; you gave me three of them already. . . ." She was still dazed, he knew; she might not be understanding all he was saying, but his words were coming in a torrent. "Sloan, I wanted the baby because I wanted to tie you to me any way that I could. I loved you since the day I met you, and that never, never changed. My pride was wounded in Belgium — and so I struck out at you, but while I was away, I knew that somehow I had to

313

keep you. Yet even having you I wasn't sure. I've been so afraid that you were still in love with Terry. . . . I was there, you see, the day that you buried him. I knew that I had to give you time. . . . I never had to come to Gettysburg; I made business here. . . ." His voice trailed away softly. "All I ever meant to do was care for you, Sloan, to make you happy, to take some of your burden from you. . . . If you want me, my wife, my sweet, sweet wife, I'll be with you."

Into her gray swirl of misery was rising a gleaming ray of incredible hope. "Terry," she murmured blankly, fighting the mind-robbing sedation. "Oh, Wes, I did love Terry. I'll never deny that. But I don't think I ever even felt for him what I do for you. I thought you weren't sure because you never seemed to plan to take me to Kentucky. . . . You were leaving alone. . . ."

"Oh, Sloan, I have been afraid, but because of you. Your life was here. I was afraid that if I took you away, you would eventually leave me. . . ."

She tried to pull him up by threading her fingers through his hair, but her strength wasn't sufficient. "Wes." He finally looked at her, moved to sit beside her on the bed. "Wes," she repeated softly, "my life is with you — wherever that is."

They stared at one another for moments of excruciating happiness, all barriers gone. They would still mourn for the child they had lost, but they would mourn together. Wes finally broke the contact, his eyes closing as he lowered his head to touch his lips against hers, lightly, gently, reverently. There was still so much to be said, but it was all inconsequential when compared to the silent love and security they had now discovered.

A throat was suddenly and very gruffly cleared from the doorway. "I'm sorry, Mr. Adams," Doc Ricter advised quietly, "but your wife absolutely has to get some rest."

"Yes, she does." Wes released her hand and stood immediately. Doc Ricter tactfully disappeared, and Wes bent to touch her lips one last time. "I'll be here first thing in the morning," he whispered against her mouth. "I love you."

Sloan savored the taste of lips that knew passion and tenderness. "I love you," she whispered back, knowing that he believed her, knowing that they would both say the words over and over during their lifetime together, and both be fully aware of the depth of the emotion that lay behind them.

Sloan closed her eyes while still feeling his touch. She was sinking into a haze, losing herself to the sleep of sedation, but his touch lingered. The pain of loss and sadness was still with her, but so much less now that it was shared. Her husband had given her rest. He had given her love; he had accepted love.

One day her sister would tell her how her giant of a man had fallen into oblivion with the fear of her loss, and she would smile with tender adoration.

But that was in the future. Now she slept with the memory of his gentle, sustaining lips against hers.

# *EPILOGUE*

As she swirled and floated with grace, with beauty, she was mercury; she was the wind, so fluid and light that she was ethereal, a goddess of the clouds upon which she appeared to hover. As always with her, she was a creature of the music, a dancer by instinct, a woman of regal beauty which the passage of time merely served to enhance.

To most who watched her, she was untouchable magic. An illusion of splendor to view, but never to capture.

And yet she had been captured, by one man in the audience.

He too was ageless. His presence would always be noted; till the day he died he would be petitioned for autographs, advice, appearances, and opinions.

It was also his name that blazed outside on the marquee. It was the prestigious Adams Dance Company that the audience had come to view, although the audience was not necessarily aware that the Adams who would be remembered as a football hero was the same who owned the dance company.

It didn't really matter.

At the performance's end, he cordially signed autographs, but his mind was not with his automatic action. He was anxious to get backstage.

She had teasingly promised him a surprise, and he had been about to go crazy even while seduced by the performance.

Backstage, she was quickly changing into street clothes, a secret smile on her lips — her mind also absent as she replied to others. She was eager to see her husband; she had marvelous news for him. Intimate, wonderful news.

Wes tapped lightly on his wife's door, then stuck his head inside. She was just brushing out her hair; her eyes met his in the mirror and she smiled. "Come in for a second," she said, dropping her brush and swirling in a circle to display the soft folds of the beige silk skirt she wore. "Like it?" she inquired.

"Umm, very much," he assured her, brows raising as she finished her twirl in his arms, planting both hands on his chest and giving him a mysterious, tantalizing smile. He caught her wrists. "Okay, minx," he charged. "I love the outfit, but why so dressy? And what's this secret? I've been going nuts the entire show."

Sloan laughed, unperturbed by his determined demand.

"I'm 'dressy,' " she informed him, "because you're taking me somewhere elegant for a late supper. And" — she ran her fingers lightly over his lapel — "after you've suitably wined and dined your hardworking wife, you'll be in on the secret."

"Un-unh," Wes shook his head. "Now."

"I'll compromise." Sloan chuckled. "As soon as you've ordered the champagne, I'll tell you."

Sloan let out a startled gasp as she felt a vise clamp on her wrist — and her feet suddenly fly across the room. "Hey!" she protested laughingly.

"I'm compromising," Wes explained patiently, "but let's get there."

With stern patience, he did wait for the champagne. Then, when the waiter had moved on, he leaned his frame over the table and his eyes challenged hers. His patience was at an end. "Okay, Sloan, out with it."

She didn't hedge a minute longer. "I'm pregnant."

She saw the frown creep into his brow, the worry and concern wrinkle his forehead. She loved him for it.

"Sloan," he began carefully, taking her fingers into his. "I'm happy, of course; you know what this means to me, but not enough to take any risks. We have three children; we've discussed this before —"

"Wes!" Sloan pressed a finger against his lips. "Don't worry, please don't worry." In a hurry to assure him, she began to trip over her words. "I've known for some time. . . . I waited to tell you to make sure. . . . Wes, I'm past the real danger point, and I had ultrasound today. Everything is fine. I promise."

He caught her hand, kissing the palm, then each finger. His eyes met hers; the love and joy she saw in their green depths were all that she would need to sustain her for a lifetime, come what may.

"When," he asked, his voice absurdly shaky.

"April." She smiled.

"Oh, Sloan," he murmured, clasping her hand to his cheek. "You have to be so very careful. I don't think I could bear the thought of losing you again —"

"I intend to be very careful," she said softly, the fingers she held moving against his cheek. Was it possible that he could love her so very much? That all their trials had come to this magnificent result? The past — the time they had spent crossing in the night but never touching — was now so worthwhile. It made their lives so infinitely more precious; it made them both realize how important it was to always value the love that they had learned to share.

Suddenly stern, Wes lowered his voice, still holding her hand, but clasping it firmly. "I don't think I've ever been happier in my life, Sloan, but this will be it — I want your promise. A son or a daughter will be wonderful — but then we will have four. No more risks, promise."

Sloan twisted her lips into a wry smile. "I'd like to promise, Wes, but —"

"No 'buts,' " he said sternly.

"Wes!" she chuckled, eyes wide. "I'm not trying to dispute you, but I can't change what already is."

"What are you talking about?"

Sloan took a moment to refill their champagne glasses. "I think you're going to need a drink," she told him sagely.

He accepted his glass from her fingers, his green gaze wary upon her face. "I have my drink."

"Well . . ." Sloan took a sip of her own champagne. "I told you I had been to the doctor . . . or did I? I'm not sure. By my own choice, not his — he says I'm as healthy as ever — I've decided to curtail the dancing

for a while. Tonight was the last performance I'll be doing with the company until
next summer —"

"Sloan," Wes interrupted, "I approve, I'm
glad to hear all this, but why do I need the
drink?"

"Because we are going to have five children," she explained with a guileless smile.
Laughing at his stunned confusion, she
lightly tapped his cheek. "Twins, Wes. We're
having twins."

"Twins." He repeated the word.

"Twins." She agreed.

"Wow," he said blankly.

"Aren't you happy?"

The slight edge of nervousness in her
voice spurred him out of his shock. Oblivious to any other patrons in the restaurant,
he inched around the booth and enveloped
her into his embrace, claiming her lips fully
with both tenderness and passion, love and
desire. Sloan had no objection. Her lips
parted beneath his as they always would, savoring his love afresh each time.

At long last he broke away. He lifted a
champagne glass to be shared between
them. "To our twins," he murmured, his
eyes caressing her with his love, "to our
family of five," he continued, his voice lowering to the husky sound of velvet she would

always thrill to, "but most of all, my darling, to you. A dream of a lifetime come true."

Wes started to sip the champagne, but Sloan held him back. "Wait a minute," she murmured, lashes lowering as she lifted the glass to him. "To you, Wes." Her eyes raised back to his. "To knights in white armor who do come along!"

"To us!" Drawing her into the firm shelter of his arm, he was finally able to sip his champagne.

The employees of Thorndike Press hope you have enjoyed this Large Print book. All our Large Print titles are designed for easy reading, and all our books are made to last. Other Thorndike Press Large Print books are available at your library, through selected bookstores, or directly from us.

For information about titles, please call:

(800) 223-1244
(800) 223-6121

To share your comments, please write:

Publisher
Thorndike Press
P.O. Box 159
Thorndike, Maine 04986